Good Pussy
Bad Pussy
in Captivity

Other books by A. Aimee

Good Pussy Bad Pussy – Rachel's Tale (2013)

Good Pussy
Bad Pussy
in Captivity

A. Aimee

Winchester, UK
Washington, USA

First published by Bedroom Books, 2015
Bedroom Books is an imprint of John Hunt Publishing Ltd., Laurel House, Station Approach,
Alresford, Hants, SO24 9JH, UK
office1@jhpbooks.net
www.johnhuntpublishing.com
www.bedroom-books.com

For distributor details and how to order please visit the 'Ordering' section on our website.

Text copyright: A. Aimee 2014

ISBN: 978 1 78279 942 9
Library of Congress Control Number: 2015932354

A CIP catalogue record for this book is available from the British Library.

Design: Lee Nash

Printed and bound in the USA by Edwards Brothers Malloy

We operate a distinctive and ethical publishing philosophy in all
areas of our business, from our global network of authors to
production and worldwide distribution.

CONTENTS

PART I

CAP FERRAT, THE FRENCH RIVIERA

Little did I know that the day my beloved, Albert, was abducted by terrorists in Jordan was also the beginning of my own captivity.

That horrendous day started innocently enough. I was sitting peacefully in the sunny glass-covered terrace connected to Albert's house on Cap Ferrat, while baby Isabella was taking her afternoon nap in her little crib beside me. Albert was away, in Amman, Jordan, heading a conference with his friend, Prince Abdul of Saudi Arabia. They were presenting their developmental project called "Reconstruction" to top Jordanian officials and members of the influential K Fund.

I had spoken to Albert on the phone a few hours earlier. The week-long conference, which was being held at the Four Seasons Hotel in downtown Amman, had ended. Albert and his team were packing up to return home in a few hours' time. I was relieved and delighted. Neither Albert nor I had been particularly happy about him going to Jordan to begin with...

That was when Victor Gandler, CEO of Albert's company, Giovanni International, knocked on the glass door of the terrace. He'd been working down in the annex offices at the lower end of the property.

I got up and opened the door.

"What's up, Victor?"

"Rachel, there's something you should know."

I motioned him to come in. I never particularly liked Victor, but since he was the leading member of Albert's team, I always did my best to be friendly and polite.

"Turn on the TV."

"Why? What's up?"

"A massive car bomb just exploded outside the Four Seasons

Hotel in Amman. Apparently just as all the delegates were leaving the hotel for the airport."

"Oh no!" I cried and ran back into the room.

I turned on the TV.

CNN. BREAKING NEWS flashed across the screen. MASSIVE EXPLOSION OUTSIDE THE FOUR SEASONS HOTEL IN AMMAN. Live pictures from outside the hotel flashed across the screen. It was mayhem... smoke was everywhere... destroyed vehicles, hysterical people in shock, screaming and staggering around... the carnage was...

All the blood seemed to drain from me and I sat down, feeling faint.

"Oh my God!" I cried.

BREAKING NEWS kept flashing across the screen.

People covered in blood were just staggering around – looking dazed and shocked. There was smoking wreckage everywhere...

BREAKING NEWS kept flashing across the screen...

* * *

Just five months before that horrendous day in mid-December, life looked completely different. Albert and I had returned to Cap Ferrat from New York and were blissfully happy. The grueling experience of Howard's trial for attacking me in the hospital and triggering baby Isabella's pre-mature birth was over at last. Howard had been sentenced to eighteen months in prison for threatening our baby's life and causing her to be born five weeks before she was due. But now she was thriving and we were finally able to go to Albert's house on Cap Ferrat and get our lives back. So we did. We packed up and flew to Nice with three-month old Isabella and my five-year-old son, Daniel.

We were elated, high and overjoyed at our good fortune.

Finally there was time for us.

Albert's house was perfect in every way, like an enchanted

ship. And there we were – Albert and I with our new baby – on a fairy-tale cruise in that big, wonderful house on the hill, overlooking the sea.

Everything was perfect.

Everything delighted us.

I savored every moment and knew Albert did too, because finally we were alone again. Finally we were able to find each other after our time of trial in New York. Isabella was a wonderful baby – easy in every way – and miracle of miracles, Albert, the love of my life, was her father!

Our first project as a family after we arrived was to redo Albert's house. Though I loved the Zen minimalist way he had decorated the house when I originally saw it the year before, moving in with him and our new baby and my son Daniel meant we had to make a lot of changes. Because it was no longer going to be the house of an eligible bachelor with a hang for open spaces and Zen meditation, but rather it was going to be "our home" – a house for our new family.

So we made changes everywhere and Albert seemed to delight in doing it. Nothing was sacred or off limits when it came to making changes. My favorite space by far in the house was the spacious glass-covered terrace which we made into a lovely living room/playroom for us and the children. It was such a wonderful room because the light was always fantastic, and you could be there all year round, no matter what the weather.

"My mother loved this room too," Albert told me, "and always wanted to sit here. You know she moved here from Vienna and lived after my father died. I always found her here whenever I came to the house."

"Well, it makes sense," I said, "if you've spent most of your life in a cold climate!"

"Exactly what she always said," he replied laughing.

We threw out all the stuff that was in there and redid the space completely, putting in large, comfy white sofas and arms chairs, and adding nice throw rugs on the floor and also on the playing space for Daniel and Isabella.

Albert kept his office on the lower level of the house with its splendid view of the Mediterranean. But the annex further down the property was where his business operations were really based. The annex, which was mostly hidden from view from the house by the trees, had several well-equipped offices, a meeting room, a luxurious lounge, and it was connected to a two-storey guest house for visitors. I was delighted with the set-up because it meant that even if Albert had to work with his team, he wasn't far away.

But now it was summer and, fortunately for us, it was a slow time of the year for Giovanni International. So we spent our time lounging around the pool; I swam a lot while Albert would sit with baby Isabella. Daniel also loved the pool, but we put him in a local playschool because we wanted him to make friends and learn French as quickly as possible.

It wasn't long after we arrived that Albert's best friend and my former lover, Stefan, came to the house with his Dutch wife, Monique, and their two daughters, Sabine and Linda.

It was a big surprise to see them.

It was also the first time I'd seen Stefan since I left him in Nice the previous October when I discovered I was pregnant.

My heart skipped a beat when I saw Stefan approaching on that hot sunny day.

"Look who's coming!" I cried out in surprise. We weren't expecting them.

Albert and I were sitting by the pool with Isabella napping beside us when suddenly, Stefan came walking across the lawn towards us with his family.

Seeing Stefan like that, all of a sudden after so long, sent an intense rush of energy through my body.

Albert jumped up to greet them! "What a wonderful

surprise!" he cried.

I just sat there, stunned. *Stefan!*

I hadn't forgotten him or how gorgeous he was or how much I loved him. I tingled all over as he approached in his white jeans and tight-fitting black t-shirt. He looked so divine. *Oh, my blond Adonis, how I loved him!*

Albert hugged Stefan and Monique warmly. Then he took Stefan's two daughters by the hand and led them quietly over to the baby carriage where Isabella was sleeping.

I got up and just stood there, gaping, drinking in Stefan with my eyes as he and his wife turned and came over to me. It was a shock to finally see his wife in real life after all that happened between Stefan and me. She was as blond and gorgeous as he was.

Did Monique know Stefan and I had been lovers? I wondered.

But there was something about her open, friendly manner that told me she didn't.

He hasn't told her, I smiled to myself. *Wise, very wise.*

So I played along and didn't immediately throw myself into his arms. Instead we just hugged in a friendly way, as friends will do who haven't seen each other in a long time. Then I shook hands with Monique and we all went over to see baby Isabella. She was awake now and looking at us with her big brown eyes.

Albert picked her up and as he did, I watched Stefan. This was the first time Stefan had actually seen the baby and the relief on his beautiful face was palpable. It was obvious she wasn't his baby! Yes, Isabella really did have curly, jet-black hair and dark brown eyes like Albert. There wasn't a trace of blond baby in her! Not a trace! It was obvious she wasn't his child as we both thought when I first discovered I was pregnant.

"She's so beautiful, Albert," Stefan said softly, touching her little cheek. "Beautiful."

I was positive Albert knew what Stefan was thinking too.

"Isn't she a little angel?" Stefan smiled, turning to his blond, blue-eyed daughters, who were both wide-eyed with appreciation.

"She looks just like you, Albert!" exclaimed Sabine, the eldest, and everyone laughed.

After that, Stefan's girls pulled off their shorts and t-shirts and hopped in the pool while we all sat down in the shade and chatted. Albert's housekeeper, Madam Raffin, came out with refreshments for everyone. It was all very relaxing and homey.

As usual, Stefan didn't say very much, but Monique chatted away.

"So you lived in Amsterdam?" she cried when I said I knew the city.

I couldn't help but smile inwardly as I listened to her talk. She was so obviously Dutch, very down-to-earth and outspoken.

"Oh yes, I lived there for seven years."

"For seven years! Really? What were you doing there?"

"I was married to a Dutchman."

"You were...?" Monique was incredulous.

"Yes, believe it or not, I was!"

Everyone laughed.

Then Monique and I exchanged a little gossip about Amsterdam, where I'd lived and where she'd lived, and a bit about the shop Jan and I had in the center of town – and also about my son, Daniel, who was at playschool.

"I would have kept Daniel home today," I said, "if I'd known you and the girls were coming."

Monique started to reply but then stopped in the middle of her sentence with this quizzical look on her face. First she looked at Albert and then at me. "But if you lived in Amsterdam, Rachel," she said slowly, looking back and forth from Albert to me, "then how in the world did the two of you meet?"

I could have sworn Stefan turned pale when she asked that question.

Obviously she didn't know it was Stefan who brought me to

the Riviera from Amsterdam and introduced me to Albert.

"Oh, now that's a very long story," I exclaimed and jumped up from my chair with the most innocent smile on my face. "Why don't we all take a swim? It's so hot today."

"Good idea," Stefan chimed in immediately, standing up and pulling off his t-shirt.

Albert just sat there, smiling like a Buddha. "You all go ahead. I'll look after Isabella."

That night in bed, Albert asked, "Well, darling, how was it to see Stefan again?"

His question took me by surprise, but I answered truthfully, "Oh it was great, just great. You know how much I loved him, and still do."

"Yes," he said slowly, "I do know. And I also know he loves you too – so much – even though he's probably never told you in so many words."

"No, he never really did," I replied. "But I guess I always knew, on some level that he did."

"He's not much of a talker and probably never will be."

"No, definitely not!" I smiled and we both laughed.

"But the truth is we both love him," I continued. "Isn't that right?"

"Yes, darling, it is. There's just something about Stefan – a kind of purity that just gets to you. Once he decides he loves you, well, his loyalty is undying. You know that."

We were both silent for a moment.

"Fortunately, Monique doesn't seem to know Stefan was with me."

"No, she doesn't, that's obvious. She wouldn't have been so relaxed and chatty if she had the slightest suspicion that the two of you were lovers."

"Well, that's a relief – it would probably make things really difficult for all of us if she knew."

"Yeah, undoubtedly," said Albert, "but you saw for yourself she's a pretty tough cookie, as you Americans say. The truth is, she hasn't always been happy with Stefan's relationship with me. She wants him to be more independent."

"So I noticed."

There was silence for a moment until I added, laughing again, "Didn't Stefan seem relieved when he finally saw with his own eyes that Isabella obviously isn't his baby."

"Yes, he did," smiled Albert. "But I don't think you realize how difficult your getting pregnant was for him."

"No... maybe not..."

"To really understand his reaction," Albert continued, "you have to know a little about his background, which I'm sure he never told you much about."

"No, not really..."

"Well, he comes from a little village in the mountains of Austria from mountain people and his family is Catholic and very religious. People like that take the matter of having children very, very seriously."

"You mean like you do!" I added, poking him in the ribs.

"Yes," he replied laughing, "... like I do. But even more so in Stefan's case because he already had two daughters when you got pregnant. You've got to remember that. And understand that he was always so troubled by the fact that his marriage to Monique was so problematic. Not so much because of his feelings for her, but because of his daughters. He feels being a father is a solemn duty so he really wants to be with his girls and be their father. That's how important it is to him."

"He did tell me, right from the beginning, how much he missed his daughters..." I said, thinking back to my short, tempestuous love affair with Stefan.

We were both silent, thinking about Stefan.

"When you think about his background," Albert continued, "you better understand that all Monique's liberal Dutch ways and talk of single parenting and mothers taking care of their children without their fathers was something he never really understood or was willing to accept."

"Hmmm…" I replied, "I guess you're right. Stefan once told me that if I didn't have a child, and if he didn't have two, he would have dropped everything and run away with me. In fact, he told me that more than once."

"Well, I'm sure he meant it and that's probably the biggest declaration of love any woman's ever gotten out of Stefan. So you should be honored, my darling. I can see I was right when I said he really did – and probably still does – love you."

"Well, maybe he does," I said teasingly as I pushed Albert down on his back so I could crawl up on top of him.

He was a sight to behold. I just loved looking at him with his slightly tousled, curly, jet-black hair and that mischievous grin on his lips. I started kissing his bare chest on my way up to his sensual mouth. I loved the warmth of his full luscious lips as my mouth bore down on his, and my hands found their way into his dark curly hair. "Hmmm…"I sighed softly as he engulfed me in his arms.

I snuggled into his chest, feeling safe and happy. We lay like that for a while, savoring our good fortune and enjoying the tranquility of being together.

Then I felt his hands slowly moving down my naked back, caressing me gently as his hands sought my buttock and thighs. "How is little pussy doing tonight?" he whispered softly in my ear. "Is she …" He didn't finish his sentence but I knew, once again, he was going to ask me how my pussy was doing now after the birthing. It wasn't the first time he'd asked.

"Oh, darling," I sighed, "I'm really quite okay… really. And she's quite okay too."

"Are you sure?"

"But of course I'm sure," I said, laughing softly into his neck. "Please, I want you to touch me… I promise you, I won't break."

Obviously Albert had never been a father before, never been with a woman who had recently given birth. "It's been more than four months now," I cried laughingly.

"Come here," I said firmly as I rolled off him onto my back, pulling him with me. I wanted him on top of me. I wanted to feel all his manhood in me.

"Not so fast," he said deliciously in my ear as he fondled my nipples which went taunt at his touch. "I want to pleasure you a little first and enjoy you…" With that he moved slowly down to my pussy. First he touched her softly with his fingers and then he began caressing her gently with his tongue.

I moaned with pleasure.

Oh, he was good, oh so good.

He kept on kissing my pussy gently until I was quivering all over. Then he stopped kissing her and massaged her softly with his fingers, putting them up me with that gentle firmness of his. I sighed deeply. He knew me so well. Knew what I liked… knew everything about me…

Then, as his fingers continued to softly caress my pussy, he moved up and kissed me on the mouth.

I was in heaven, opening up under his soft, sensual touch.

"Oh, Albert," I cried, clutching his hair in my hands. "Please…" His touch was so exquisite, so knowing, so gentle, yet firm. He knew exactly how to lead me on… and on…

Then he went down on me again, teasing the tender lips of my pussy until I was gasping with delight, overtaken once more by the liquid desire he always awakened in me.

I was just about to come.

As my hips swayed, he cried, "Wait, darling, wait!" and came up for air.

Then he climbed back on top of me so I felt his erection moving up and finding my wet, waiting pussy. I was aching, aching for him, aching for him to enter her, enter me.

"Please Albert… I don't think I can wait much longer…"

And enter me, he did.

When he was deep inside me, I moaned with pleasure, having him there where I wanted him to be – at the very heart of me.

And just when I thought it couldn't get any more intense, he took my head in his hands and said, "Look at me, darling! Look at me. I want to see you come. Come to me!"

So I did, and opening my eyes, I heard myself moaning with delight as he found my depths and moved in me in that powerful, rhythmic, sensual way of his that always brought me to that ecstatic state of liquid rapture which rolled over me like warm waves from a gentle, loving ocean.

It was pure, unadulterated bliss.

Then the moment came, like a shattering explosion when I imploded around him. Coming because I simply couldn't wait any longer, couldn't hold back the intensity of feeling he'd aroused in me, couldn't. So I surrendered to the shuddering waves and let myself go, looking into his deep, dark eyes, looking at the man I loved and adored, looking... and I came so hard and fast, so powerfully and mightily, that my world thundered down and enfolded round him.

And he joined me there, once again, as was his way. Meeting me with perfect timing! Yes, he was there, holding me, caressing and taking me ever deeper and higher. Drawing out the moment as he found my depths and we delighted in the pleasure of it, the ecstasy and intensity of it, as it brought us together, taking us to our very own place, to our very own, glorious place... where sex and love joined together in life's most sacred prayer...

So the days passed, blissful days with Albert... and I felt myself reviving and coming alive again, sharing my life with this wonderful man.

And as we frolicked, I realized that good pussy bad pussy was back too! Back! Yes she was! And it was great to feel her alive in me again, alive, reviving and lusting for life! After all we'd been through. She and

I. She loved the moment of it, she loved the sex of it, she loved the me of it, she loved the….

One day in early December, when Albert came up from his office on the lower level of the house for lunch, he didn't look especially happy. Usually our lunch together with Isabella was one of the highlights of our day. Albert simply doted on her. Obviously they had a very special bond.

When he came up, he always did the same thing – he'd tickle her tiny feet until she was giggling with delight. It was their little ritual. But on that day, he didn't.

I could see she was sitting there, in her high chair, waiting for him to come in and start tickling her, but he just stood in the doorway, looking solemnly at us both.

"Anything wrong, sweetheart?" I asked, wiping Isabella's mouth. She started kicking her little feet as if she was asking him why he wasn't tickling her.

"I have to go to Jordan for a conference," he said tersely, still standing in the doorway.

"Oh," I felt my stomach drop.

Neither of us spoke for a while. He still didn't move.

"Why do you have to go?"

When he didn't answer I said, "When? When do you have to go?"

"Day after tomorrow."

"Oh no!"

He came in and pulled up a chair and sat down next to Isabella, but he still didn't tickle her feet even though she kept kicking them as if she was trying to get his attention. She was eight months old and already had quite a mind of her own.

"So why do you have to go?" I asked again, breaking the silence.

"I just spoke to Prince Abdul of Saudi Arabia. He's an old friend of mine. It seems a project we've been working on for the last couple of years is suddenly coming to fruition and is about to be approved by the Jordanian government."

"Really? What project?"

"It's called *Reconstruction*. I don't think I ever told you about it."

"No, I don't think you ever did...*Reconstruction*... What is it?"

"Well, it's a complex and ambitious relocation plan the Prince and I developed a couple of years ago. Designed to help poor refugees out of those dismal refugee camps and provide them with the opportunity to build new lives and communities where people can cultivate the land – by using machinery supplied by Giovanni International at a very low cost."

"Oh, I see... sounds like a great idea."

"It is, but the plan's been stalled for ages because it can only work if it's approved and backed financially by the Jordanian government since they're one of the major stakeholders in all this and must allocate land for this purpose. To be honest, we'd kind of given up hope of it ever coming to fruition.

"But now the Prince tells me several top-level officials and other highly influential people in the region, including the K Fund are putting pressure on some of the king's senior advisors. So it suddenly looks like the Jordanian government is ready to move forward on this."

He was silent for a moment.

"Do you really have to go?" Everything in me was saying *No! No! You can't go away now. Not yet, we just got here. It's way too soon.*

The room was silent.

Isabella stopped kicking her little feet and was watching us with her big brown eyes.

Everything about his body language told me he didn't want to go.

"It's my project..." he said slowly.

The night before he was leaving, Albert pulled me to him in our big bed and said, "Rachel, let's get married."

I was shocked by the suddenness of his words and just sat there, stunned.

"Married?" I said finally, and let the word slide lowly across my tongue.

The idea of marrying Albert had never occurred to me.

"Yes, darling," he said, smiling gently at me, "married."

"But I already am married," I said, laughing and pulling myself away from him. I sat up cross-legged and looked at him, puzzled.

"Yes, I know," he said, propping himself up on his elbow, "but soon you'll be divorced. And then we can get married. I want you to be my wife."

"Married," I let the word slide slowly across my lips again, "But why? Why do we need to get married?" It seemed like such a strange idea to me. Then the words just flew out of my mouth, "Oh Albert, you know the love we share has nothing to do with a piece of paper!"

Albert laughed too and sat up. He was naked and lovely to look at. "You really are my little miracle! Do you have any idea how many women have wanted to marry me? And always for the wrong reasons. Either it was for my money or for the prestige of landing someone like me, or just for my good looks and connections." He laughed again. "And you, the first woman I've ever truly loved and wanted to marry – you don't even care."

I couldn't help but laugh with him; he was so sweet in all his earnestness.

"But Albert, it's true what I'm saying. I've already been married so I know very well that love has nothing to do with marriage. And besides, I don't want to own you. I just want to keep on playing with you, my darling. That's all I want."

"Oh we will, we will. I promise you we'll continue playing," he replied solemnly. "But what I was actually thinking was that I want to give Isabella my name legally so that if anything happens to us – she will inherit my fortune. And I also want to protect you, my darling, if anything should happen to me."

I shuddered at the thought.

"Albert, dearest," I cried, not wanting to think like that. Just the thought of something happening to him made me go cold all over, but then I realized he was deadly serious.

"When I get back from Jordan, I am going to talk to my lawyer about remaking my will, so my estate will go to you and Isabella if anything happens to me – whether or not you agree to marry me."

He spoke with such conviction that all I could do was listen in silence, not realizing how prophetic his words would turn out to be…

When he saw me looking so serious, he suddenly got this mischievous twinkle in his eye and said, "But there is something I want to give you before I go." He got up from the bed and began fishing in the big dresser drawer where I kept my papers and our passports. "Now close your eyes and put out your hands."

"What is it?"

"It's just a little present. Now just do what I say."

"Albert," I cried. "What is it?"

"Just close your eyes…"

I did as he said and felt him drop some keys into my hand.

I opened my eyes. "Why, these are the keys to the loft in Soho. But I already have the keys," I said, not understanding.

"I know you do, darling, but you didn't have this before," he said, pulling an envelope out from behind his back and giving it to me.

"What is it?" I said, opening the envelope and looking at the papers but not understanding what they were.

"It's the deed to the apartment. I've had the documents made over – so now the loft belongs to you. It's all paid for and now you own it outright. Legally it's yours."

"Oh, Albert," I cried, "You don't need to do this."

"I know," he said softly, "but I want to."

When I didn't say anything, he continued, his eyes twinkling, "When you go back to New York next year to go to school, maybe you'll let me come along and stay with you."

* * *

Just eight short days later I was sitting in shock in front of the TV staring at the words BREAKING NEWS: MASSIVE EXPLOSION OUTSIDE THE FOUR SEASONS HOTEL IN AMMAN as they flashed across the screen.

The words just kept on flashing, over and over again.

BREAKING NEWS: MASSIVE EXPLOSION OUTSIDE THE FOUR SEASONS HOTEL IN AMMAN

I felt my world reeling.

The pictures of the carnage in front of the hotel were appalling. Blood-covered people were staggering around in the mayhem.

What if Albert's been seriously injured?

What if...

What if he's been killed...?

What if he's... dead...?

I felt faint.

The room seemed to fade in and out of my consciousness.

I felt hot all over.

I was aware of Victor holding my hand. "Rachel, we don't know anything yet."

"But... what... do you think?" I gasped, trying to focus. "What if he's dead?"

"Rachel, we don't know anything yet. We don't even know if Albert was there at the time."

I felt like I couldn't breathe.

"But what can we do?"

That was when I remembered my phone. I picked it up and frantically pressed Albert's number.

Answer! Please answer!

The automatic voice recording said there was no connection to his number at the time.

"Oh no," I cried. "His phone isn't working. It says there's no connection..."

Now the tears were flowing.

"I just talked to him a couple of hours ago. He said he was packing up to come home."

I couldn't get my head around it.

"What if he's dead... what if...?" I cried.

"Rachel, please, we don't know anything yet," Victor repeated. "Please, you must be calm, my dear."

"Calm!" I almost screamed, "But I don't feel calm. How can I feel calm..." My mind was reeling.

"I just didn't want you to be taken by surprise if someone official or someone from the media calls you. We don't know anything yet."

I was shaking all over.

I tried to focus on the TV screen.

It was horrendous to look at. There was blood and carnage everywhere and it certainly looked like a lot of people had been killed or seriously injured. But the blast had literally just happened so nobody seemed to have any idea what was going on. The CNN team had obviously been close by in the hotel covering the conference Albert was hosting with Prince Abdul. Which explained why they were on the scene so fast...

Oh my God! Where is Albert... Albert... where are you?

Maybe I would see him... but I didn't... All I could see were lots of people staggering around covered with blood – looking dazed and traumatized. The emergency services were starting to arrive and a few bewildered policemen were trying to clear a path for the first responders to come through.

I put my head in my hands and wept. Little Isabella woke up in all the commotion and started crying too.

Victor went and got Amélie, our nanny, and asked her to take Isabella and get someone to pick up Daniel at his playschool. It was three in the afternoon. I hardly noticed what was going on.

Then Victor called Stefan and Monique and asked them to come over right away.

Two hours later, after repeated calls to the Foreign Ministry and the Four Seasons Hotel in Amman, Victor had some news. He put down the phone as Stefan, Monique, and I listened.

"There's no news about Albert," he said quietly. "None whatsoever. They simply don't know anything about his whereabouts yet. He doesn't seem to be among the dead or injured. And he's not in the hotel either. No one knows where he is."

I buried my head in my hands.

There was a long silence.

Victor was pacing the floor.

"But they say Joey has been killed by the blast," he continued, "and so has Albert's technical assistant, Gerald Rainer. They are both confirmed dead."

"Oh no," I looked up and cried in horror, "poor Joey!" Joey was Albert's driver, the young fellow from North Africa I met at the very first party at Albert's house I had attended. The party Stefan took me to almost one and a half years ago when I first came to the Rivera with him.

"But what about Albert?" I cried in despair. "Where can he be? What's happened to him?"

"They simply don't know, Rachel," Victor said. "All we can do right now is wait."

"Oh God… please … let him be okay…" I cried. "… Please…"

There was nothing more to say.

Monique and Stefan were sitting on either side of me, holding my hands.

And so we sat.

After a while, Monique got up and went to help Amélie with Daniel and Isabella.

Stefan put his arm around me and held me tight. Victor went back to the annex to make more calls. "If I find out anything, I'll be right back."

It was six hours later that we got confirmation from the Foreign Ministry that Albert was definitely not among the dead or injured. In fact, he was not there at all and simply couldn't be accounted for. Everyone else was accounted for, but not Albert. No one had seen him or knew where he was.

At two in the morning, Albert's close friend, Prince Abdul of Saudi Arabia, called. Victor put the Prince on the speakerphone so we could all hear what he had to say.

"I was still in my suite when the attack took place so I didn't see anything," the Prince explained. "But I have been talking to the various officials who are now in involved here and we all agree that in all probability, Albert has been abducted."

"Abducted!" Stefan, Monique, Victor and I gasped in unison.

I felt the room go out of focus.

Abducted? My mind was screaming. *Abducted? What does this mean?*

"Well, yes," said the Prince, "abducted… He was an obvious, easy target, being a wealthy Western business man in the Middle East with no security team around him."

There was a hushed silence as we all tried to digest this new information.

"The authorities here believe – and I agree with them – that the car bomb was probably just a decoy, a diversion – designed to cause enough chaos to allow the terrorists to grab Albert and whisk him away without being detected."

There was a grim silence in the room until the Prince continued, "Obviously, since Albert was such a high profile target, it would be difficult to get him out of Amman undetected unless there was a serious diversion to occupy the attention of the authorities."

Albert abducted! Could it be true?

At three in the morning, an official from the Foreign Ministry in Paris called and asked to speak to Albert's nearest associates and family members. Again, Victor put the speakerphone on and then proceeded to introduce us to Jacques Durand, the special assistant to the Foreign Minister who had been assigned to handle this case.

"I apologize for not calling back sooner, but I didn't want to call until we were absolutely certain that Albert is not among the dead or injured. And I can assure you now – he is not.

"So we are now operating on the assumption that Albert has been kidnapped," Durand continued.

"What does that mean?" I cried, feeling exhausted and hysterical.

"And you are?" Durand asked.

"Rachel... Rachel Somers..."

"Oh yes, I understand you are Albert's partner... is that correct?"

"Yes. We have an eight-month old daughter..."

"Well, Rachel, when rich businessmen are kidnapped by fanatics in the region, it's always for one reason and one reason alone – and that's money. Money to finance their operations. In their minds, kidnapping rich businessmen is a fast and easy way to achieve this end.

"So in this case, we expect it will mean the abductors will be asking – and asking very soon – for a ransom for Albert's release, which, in all likelihood, will be a very substantial amount."

I felt my heart pounding in my chest.

Albert is being held for ransom by terrorists! Held for RANSOM!

"In all probability," Durand continued, "we can expect to be contacted by his kidnappers very shortly."

"Who will they contact?" Victor asked, "And how?"

"Well, they operate in different ways. But in most cases, they will either contact the government or the relevant embassy involved through one of their intermediaries in the region – or they might try contacting you directly at Giovanni International. I cannot tell you exactly how this will play out. But one thing I can tell you for sure, we will be contacted one way or the other, if money is their aim."

When no one said anything, he continued, "Even though, as you probably know, the official government policy in France and throughout Europe is that governments don't pay ransom, it is a well-known fact that companies, and some governments, do."

But of course, we'll pay the ransom my mind was screaming.*Of course, I don't care how much it is!*

Again silence.

Durand cleared his throat. "For the moment, there is really nothing more we can do – except wait. So for the time being, I suggest that everyone go to bed and try to get some sleep. It's been a very long day for all of us."

I started to cry.

I just couldn't hold it in anymore.

When Durand heard me crying in the background, his voice softened and he said, "Rachel, you must take comfort in the fact that since groups like this are only interested in money, and lots of it – it means that in all probability Albert is alive and well. You must remember this. If something happens to Albert, they're not going to get what they want... Just remember that the only way they can achieve their goal is to take relatively good care of him... and deliver him back to us safely... "

I buried my face in my hands and wept.

Stefan put his arm around me, and Monique held my hand as I wept.

"What can we expect to happen next?" Victor stood up and asked.

"Well, what will probably happen is some days will pass until we are all feeling very desperate. And then, when they think enough time has passed and that we are desperate enough, they will contact us – through one channel or another – and ask us to pay a ransom.

"If we agree, then we will be given precise instructions as to how, when and where we are to deliver the money. Often militant groups like this stipulate that the money should be dropped somewhere really remote and difficult to find, so I suggest that if they contact you directly at Giovanni International, you work together with me and the French government to try to arrange these matters as quickly and efficiently as we can, so we are able to get Albert released as fast as possible."

Monique and Stefan were the last to leave. They took me up to bed and sat with me until they simply couldn't keep their eyes open. It was four thirty-five in the morning.

"Go on home," I whispered. "Go… I'll call you tomorrow…"

Finally they left.

I crumpled up in a big ball in our bed and wept.

Albert abducted! ABDUCTED!

I simply couldn't get my head around it.

How could it be?

My beloved, Albert, abducted by terrorists! And held for ransom!

Sleep was impossible.

How could this have happened?

Oh God, where was he?

How was he?

Was he hurt?

How were they treating him?

It didn't bear thinking about. I needed something or someone to hold on to. I called my mother in New York. Because of the six-hour time difference, I knew she would still be up. I'd already spoken to her earlier in the day when the news first broke.

When she picked up the phone, I wailed, "Oh, Momma! Now

they're sure he's been kidnapped – and being held for ransom!"

"Oh my God," she whispered softly.

"Yes... abducted."

There was a long silence while I wept.

"How could this have happened?" I wailed. "How..." I was hysterical.

"Now, now, now," she whispered soothingly. "How do they know he's been kidnapped?"

When I didn't reply, she said, "Now just try to calm down a little, Rachel... come darling... take a few deep breaths..."

I did as she said.

When she heard I wasn't weeping so hysterically, she said, "Come now... tell me what they said... who did you talk to?"

I dried my nose. "We talked to the Saudi Prince – you know Albert's friend, Prince Abdul – and then we talked to Jacques Durand from the Foreign Ministry. He's the one who has been assigned to handle Albert's case. Both Jacques Durand and the Prince said the same. They both said it fits the pattern – that fanatical militant groups often kidnap wealthy Western businessmen because they're looking for ways to finance their operations.

"Albert was an easy target they say... because he didn't have a security team around him... oh, Momma! Why didn't he have a security team around him... why..."

Now I was crying again.

"They even think the bomb blast outside the hotel was just a diversion so they could kidnap Albert and whisk him away without anyone noticing it..."

"Oh, my darling..." my mother said slowly.

"Do you think he's okay, Momma? Oh Momma, I don't know what to do or think... I feel like I'm going crazy... Can't you fly over? Momma! Please fly over tomorrow... please! I need you to be here with me..."

There was a long silence.

"You know I'd come in a minute, Rachel... if I could..."

There was another long silence.

"You know I would... But since Marlene's suicide attempt, I just don't dare leave her alone – not yet... you know that..."

It was true, I did know. After the trauma of her husband Howard's trial for attacking me in the hospital and his conviction, Marlene had a nervous breakdown and tried to kill herself. She'd been in a private psychiatric facility for a while but was recently released. At the moment, she was under my mother's care, living in my mother's house. According to my mother, it was touch and go with her mental stability.

"Yes... I know..." I said and wept some more. "I just wish you could come, Momma..."

"I know, I know, my darling..." my mother sighed, "but your sister's fallen apart completely... I don't even dare leave her alone to go to the supermarket... it's that bad..."

"Oh, Momma..."

There was a long silence.

"What else did they say, Rachel?"

"They said the kidnappers would soon be contacting us and asking for a huge amount of money in exchange for his release..."

"Well, that must be a good thing..." my mother said slowly. "It must mean... " Her voice trailed off.

"Yes, I know... that's what Jacques Durand said. He said I should take comfort in the fact that these madmen have to keep Albert alive if they are going to get their money..."

The first week or two after Albert was abducted seemed to pass like in a dream – or rather, like in a nightmare. The kidnappers didn't make contact with us or the authorities until almost three weeks had passed. And the waiting was pure hell. It just seemed to go on forever. And there wasn't anything I, or anyone else, could do, except wait. Wait for word. Wait for a sign of life. Wait for something hopeful to happen. So that's what we all did;

Stefan, Monique, Victor, and the rest of the team and family around Albert, we all hunkered down and waited. Victor and Stefan were in daily contact with the Foreign Ministry and Jacques Durand, but it didn't help. They were also in touch with Prince Abdul who promised he was working all his channels to find Albert. But nothing happened. There was no sign – no word – nothing.

Sometimes at night, when I couldn't sleep, I'd roam around Albert's big house like a restless animal. But no matter where I turned or looked, Albert was always there. His energy was everywhere – in every nook and cranny. Then one night, in the middle of the night, when I had wandered downstairs to his office, I found myself sitting on the very couch where I'd first sat with him, the very first time I came to the house. Just the thought of it – just the thought of that wonderful man and what had happened to him – made me burst out crying.

My beloved Albert... abducted by terrorists... and now lost in the cauldron of the Middle East...

Albert! Albert, please be okay! Please come home!

A terrible wave of grief, anguish and anger washed over me... *It's just not fair... it's just not...Why, oh why did this happen? Why... why?* But almost immediately I heard my mother's voice saying... *It is useless to go down that path, Rachel... useless. It's useless to try and figure out why this happened... useless.* So I jumped up, wiped my eyes, and took a deep breath – and then I walked over to the door that led to Albert's meditation room.

I opened the door and stepped into the quiet room with sliding glass doors that opened out onto the sloping terrace that ran down to the Mediterranean below. The room was almost empty; all it contained were some meditation cushions, a few small, low, black-lacquered tables with exquisite bonsai on them, and a tiny altar. This was the space where he meditated everyday and where I had often joined him since our return to Cap Ferrat. I went over to the altar and lit a few candles.

A worn, black and white photo of his master Okumara Sensei was on the altar.

There was a profound silence in the room – a silence that was deep and comforting. I sat down on one of the cushions on the floor and tried to focus on my breathing. It was difficult to do because my mind was in such turmoil. But almost immediately, it was as if I heard Albert's voice in my head saying... *Rachel... Just let everything be... just let it be... and watch your breath.*

So I tried... to just notice my breathing... breath in, breath out... in and out... and then, in the profound silence, it really did feel as if Albert was there with me. His presence was so strong that it felt like he was standing right there in the room, saying to me... *Keep your spirits high, Rachel, and know deep in your heart that I am coming home to you again, my darling! No matter how long it takes...*

No matter how long...

And so the days passed, one day after the next.

Three weeks later, we had a call from Jacques Durand.

Only Victor and I were present when he called. We were sitting in Victor's office down in the annex when the call came. Victor turned on the speakerphone so we both could hear him.

"People claiming they are intermediaries for Albert's captors contacted the French authorities in Yemen yesterday," Durand said.

I felt my heart skip a beat.

"Oh, that's great!" I cried, jumping up from the chair I was sitting on.

"What more did they say?" Victor asked.

"Well, we don't have much to go on yet. All they would say is that they had knowledge of the whereabouts of one Albert Giovanni and that his captors were asking for five million Euros in exchange for his release.

Victor whistled. "That's a lot of money..."

"Yes," said Durand. "But I am not surprised. I told you it would be like this. In fact, I expected it would be in the neighborhood of this amount, considering how successful Giovanni International is…"

"But this must be good news," I exclaimed, pacing back and forth excitedly in front of the speakerphone. "Isn't it, Jacques?"

"Well, yes it is, Rachel," replied Durand. "It is… very good news… indeed. Now finally, we have someone to talk to – and can begin the negotiations and the process of getting Albert released."

I was so thrilled with the news that I ran up to the house as soon as we were done talking to Durand and called my mother.

"Momma! The kidnappers have finally made contact!"

"Oh, Rachel," she cried in delight. "That's just wonderful, my darling! What happened?"

"Well, I'm not exactly sure… but Jacques Durand just called and said people claiming they were acting as intermediaries for Albert's captors contacted the French authorities in Yemen… oh, Momma, do you think this means he'll soon be released?"

"Well, let's hope so. What else did he say?"

"He said they were asking for five million Euros in ransom…"

"Rachel, I'm not an expert in these matters, but it certainly sounds like a good sign."

"Yes, that's what he said – that now finally they have someone to talk to… "

"Oh I'm so glad," she replied. "You see, darling, it's just as I said it would be… everything is going to work out fine in the end…"

But it was slow going again after that.

After that first initial contact, there was silence again for many weeks. And it became more and more difficult for me to keep the faith…

Sometimes in the afternoon when Isabella was napping, I'd

leave her with Amélie and go down to the annex to see if Victor had any news. Now that Albert was missing, Victor had moved into the guest house and was working in the annex offices, overseeing the operations of Giovanni International from Cap Ferrat as Albert used to do.

One day, Victor rang for Madam Raffin to bring us some tea as soon as I entered his office. It seemed he wanted to talk.

After she left, he looked at me and said, "I'm afraid there's no news, Rachel."

A heavy silence descended on the room. I wondered what Victor wanted to talk about.

"In a strange way," he said, "this reminds me of the time when Albert had gone off to meditate in that Zen monastery in Japan when he was young," Victor stirred his tea and began sipping it slowly.

"What do you mean?"

"Oh, I was just thinking of how everyone missed him so much back then. Just like you do now..."

I thought I detected a hint of bitterness in his voice.

"I didn't know you had been a part of Giovanni International for so long..."

"Oh yes, Albert's father, Bernardo, hired me while Albert was gone."

"Oh, I see. So you knew his father well?"

"Yes I did. Albert was gone for almost four years..."

"I know, he told me..."

"His absence made his father furious. You see, Bernardo was a very strict man and very conservative. He was infuriated that Albert, his only son, had simply 'abandoned' the family – as he put it – to go off to some exotic Buddhist monastery in Japan and meditate all day long. He thought his son should have been home in Vienna, learning the ropes. In fact, Bernardo was so enraged at the time that he sometimes talked about disowning his son. But I always counseled him to wait, saying I knew Albert would come back, even though at that time, I'd never even met Albert."

Hearing him talk about Albert like that made me miss him so much that I burst out crying.

"Now, now, Rachel," Victor said, moving closer to me on the couch where we were sitting. "I am sure we will get him back. It's just a matter of time."

He put his arm around me and began stroking my hair.

I pulled away from him instinctively. There was something about his manner that didn't feel right.

"Of course, you're right," I said, quickly drying my eyes and trying to cover up the fact that I'd pulled away from him so demonstrably. "I know I shouldn't be crying like this, Victor, I'm sorry."

There was an uncomfortable silence. I really didn't like the man.

"I'd best go up and see to Isabella." I said, standing up and heading for the door. "Thanks for the tea, Victor."

Once outside, I felt sick inside.

Did what I think just happened, happen? Or was it just my imagination?

I shivered all over.

There was just something about the way Victor stroked my hair.

But what about it? Even if it made me feel uncomfortable, I knew I needed to stay on friendly terms with him. It was important. Not only was he my main source of information; he was in charge of Albert's company now. He was running the whole show...

Later that night as I lay in our big bed, I started thinking about Victor again and realized that this wasn't the first time Victor had tried to touch me. I'd just been so distressed about Albert's abduction that I hadn't really noticed it before.

The thought sent a chill through me. There was just something about the man that made me feel uncomfortable.

There was just something about the way he looked at me... he had those hungry eyes...

I'd better watch out... I thought... *and be more careful.*

But it happened again, a week or two later, right after Victor and I had another talk with Jacques Durand about the difficulties of maintaining contact with the people who were holding Albert. This wasn't the first time we'd had this conversation with Jacques.

"At the moment," Jacques was saying, "the situation is simply so volatile in Yemen, and in the whole region, that it's making our work very difficult. As I said before, we have been trying to set up a timeframe for the exchange of prisoner for money... but unfortunately, we're not having much success."

"Oh," I cried in dismay "has something changed? I thought you said things were going pretty much according to plan."

"Well, yes, I did say that," replied Jacques, clearing his throat. "But... you see... now hostilities have broken out between the faction that is holding Albert and the faction that seems to be rising in power in the very same area. I am afraid this is making our work very tricky – to say the least. It was difficult enough before, but now... well... they keep moving around, and well... I wish I had better news for you, Rachel, but I don't."

I just sat there, stunned.

When the conversation was over, the tears came. I simply couldn't hold them back. Victor came over with some tissues. Then he sat down on the couch next to me and put his arm around me.

I didn't want him to and wiped my eyes, saying, "Thanks, Victor. It's okay. I'll be okay. I just have to get my bearings."

"Why won't you let me comfort you, Rachel?" he replied. "Just let me hold you a little."

"No, Victor," I said, getting up from the couch. "I don't think it's a good idea... I really don't..."

"Oh, Rachel," he said as I got up, "you don't have to be so

afraid of me. I'm not going to hurt you."

I didn't know what to say, so I just turned and got out of there as fast as I could.

It was the end of June, and more than six months since Albert had been abducted, when my white iPhone rang in my pocket. When I heard the voice, I knew immediately it was Jacques Durand.

"Rachel?" he asked as my heart pounded in my chest. Jacques had never called me on my private phone before. I'd always talked to him with Victor down at the annex.

"Do you have news?" I cried.

"No, Rachel, not really."

There was an eerie silence.

"Then why are you calling?"

"Actually I am calling to tell you, Rachel... that you must prepare yourself for the worst."

When I heard these words, I felt all the blood draining out of me and I sat down on the nearest chair.

"So you do have news..." I said softly.

"No, not in that way."

"Well... then what do you mean? I mean... why are you saying this to me? What's happened?" I felt the hysteria rising in my chest, reaching up to my throat.

"Well, the thing is, we've simply lost all track of Albert and his kidnappers. The people we've been talking to... well, they've just vanished."

There was that eerie silence again.

"But... last time we spoke, you said you expected to be negotiating with the kidnappers again soon. You said the situation had calmed down a bit, so you were hopeful."

When Jacques didn't reply, I continued, "You know Giovanni International has the money and is willing to pay... haven't you spoken to Victor?"

"Yes, Rachel, of course I have, and yes, I did say that the last time we spoke because that was my expectation. I was more hopeful at the time. But now, suddenly, we've lost all contact with them. They've simply disappeared... completely... It's like the well has dried up. Up until now, we had been talking to them on and off and were trying to make arrangements for the delivery of the five million Euros as agreed. But all of a sudden, we've lost all contact with them. Our channels, our contacts, it's all a complete blank. It's like they've disappeared from the face of the earth. We were talking through channels in Yemen and were relatively certain that they'd taken Albert to one of their hideouts there because that's what these groups usually do and we had strong evidence that this was the case... but now we're not even sure about that..."

There was another long silence.

I felt my heart pounding in my chest. The room seemed to sway.

"Are you saying he's dead?"

"No Rachel, I'm not saying that. But I am saying it doesn't look good. Because it doesn't. And I'm also saying that we, at the Ministry, don't like what's happening. Because we have quite a lot of experience with these matters and suddenly things are not going the way they usually do. Usually we keep the conversation going through our intermediaries, as I told you before, and this is always extremely important. But now it's stopped completely. The lines of communication have gone dead and I don't want to keep you in the dark about this. I promised you, Rachel, from the very beginning that I would be honest and keep you informed and that's what I'm doing."

The tears were running down my cheeks and I was shaking all over.

"I see..." was all I could say.

"Rachel," Jacques' voice was softer now. "Of course you can, and should, keep on hoping – but I just want you to prepare yourself. Do you understand what I'm saying?"

"Yes, Jacques," I whispered. "I think so…"

"Well, call me if you want to talk. You have my direct number."

"Okay," was all I could say.

The phone went dead.

Oh, Albert! Albert! I felt myself screaming inside. *You can't be dead, you can't be!*

I ran upstairs to our bedroom and threw myself onto the bed, sobbing.

Oh, Albert! Albert! I felt myself screaming inside. *You can't be dead, you can't be!*

I curled up into a ball on the bed and sobbed… and sobbed…

Up until then, I had hope. Up until then, I had been telling myself it was just a matter of time. Things would work themselves out, Giovanni International would pay the money, and Albert would be freed. That was the way it worked. Everyone said so. The government had done it many times before in similar cases where rich businessmen had been taken hostage, so why shouldn't they do the same in Albert's case?

But the region was in such turmoil. Every day new groups were arising and one group was more fanatic than the next. Nobody could keep track of them all. Moreover, the various groups and splinter groups were also fighting among themselves. Who knew what was really going on?

And now the Foreign Ministry was saying I should prepare myself! Did they know more than they were telling me? Why was Jacques saying this now… now all of a sudden… that I should prepare myself? What did he know that I didn't know? What wasn't he telling me?

I curled up tighter and cried harder.

Amélie, the children's nanny, came into the room and said softly she'd put the children to sleep. I hardly noticed her…

Hours later, I called Stefan. I had to talk to someone I loved, see someone I loved, someone I trusted, someone who I felt close to, someone who understood me, someone nearby... someone...

"Stefan," I said into the phone, my voice was hoarse from so much crying, "can you come over right now? Jacques Durand from the Foreign Ministry called..."

"Sure," Stefan said even though it was very late. "Actually I was planning on coming by tomorrow anyway... Monique and the girls left for Amsterdam this morning to visit her parents and stay with family and friends for a couple of weeks..."

When Stefan arrived, I threw myself into his arms and sobbed and sobbed.

It was very late and the house was quiet. The children were sleeping and Amélie had gone to bed too.

Stefan led me to the glass-covered terrace and closed the shades. We sat down on one of the big white sofas.

"What happened?" he said, pushing back my hair.

"Jacques said I had to prepare myself for the worst!"

Stefan didn't say anything. He just held me while I cried.

"What if he's dead?" I sobbed. "What if he really is dead?"

Stefan held me tight and stroked my hair.

"Ah, Rachel..."

Several hours later I woke up, curled up in Stefan's arms. We were both lying on the big white sofa. I turned and looked over at the clock ticking softly on the wall. It was four in the morning. Stefan stirred and pulled me back to him, sighing softly. I let him, and lay very close to him and listened to the sound of his breathing. It was nice, so nice and warm and comforting, to snuggle into his warm body. He was Stefan. Stefan! The man I had loved madly. The man I still loved. He was the man I'd run off with – the man I left my first husband, Jan, to be with. The man who gave me to Albert! Yes...he was Stefan. He was...

Now he was stirring and enfolding me in his strong arms.

Half awake, half asleep, it was suddenly like old times.

Suddenly it was there again. The deliciousness of Stefan and Rachel, arising out of the ashes of this terrible despair.

Yes, it was there! The sudden rush, the sudden passion. He was kissing me and kissing me passionately, and I found myself kissing him back, with a huge hunger that amazed me.

Oh, Stefan! Stefan!

He was unbuttoning my blouse and my bra; awake now, his warm hands finding my breasts, caressing and fondling my nipples, touching my body with an undeniable knowingness... touching me.

And it was oh so delicious.

I knew, felt, loved that he remembered every inch of me and knew every curve of my body. I was still his and he was still mine – it was that obvious. And it was because of the amazing bond of love between the three of us, between Albert and Stefan and me, that this could happen. That we could feel like this now. It was as if there could be no closed doors between us, no jealousy, no possessiveness, no... just an openness and a generosity of spirit... just...

Oh, Stefan... I heard myself sighing softly, ever so softly.

Stefan hadn't touched me since the very last time we were together right before I left Nice that October morning almost two years ago....And now he was here with me again. Touching me.

Oh, Stefan! My blond Adonis!

As the hunger rose in me, I also realized that I hadn't been with a man since Albert was abducted more than six months ago... and I was so hungry... so hungry, aching... my pussy was aching, aching.

What is more, I was longing too, longing for oblivion, longing to disappear from the pain and sorrow of our lives into Stefan's white hot passion for me. For it was still there – it was. Nothing had changed. Nothing...

Once we were both naked, Stefan did what he always did. He positioned himself over me with his arms outstretched as if he was about to do push-ups. But this time, he paused for a long moment and sighed and lingered as he surveyed my waiting body with such tenderness that it almost broke my heart. Tears sprang out of the corners of my eyes; the love was that intense. His love for me and for Albert...

Then he lowered his firm body slowly down upon me, touching me gently as I closed my eyes in a swoon. He knew I liked it like that – of course he remembered. Of course he remembered I liked it when he teased me with the gentle touch of his exquisite body until I was wet and ready.

So everything was exactly as it was meant to be.

His lovemaking, so different from Albert's, was powerful in a way that only Stefan could be. And yes, there it was – that hypnotic, rhythmic dance of his which was slow, strong and silent... the wondrous wave that was Stefan.

And there I was, wet, wet, wet, ready, yielding, just as it always had been between him and me.

Oh, Stefan! Stefan! It's been so long and nothing's changed. Nothing.

It was as if we had traveled back in time to a land we once inhabited.

So I closed my eyes in a swoon as he entered me with such fierce determination that I almost cried out. But then I settled into the energy as I felt him strong and powerful within me, just as it always had been with him. Then he pressed himself deep into me, moving slowly and powerfully. Moving, moving into me as the rhythm of his body, the rhythm of his lovemaking began to gain momentum. I heard myself moaning with pleasure and sighing at the loveliness of him, at the loveliness of this wonderful and terrible moment of finding each other again – after so long – after such...*Aaahhh*... and I knew with a terrible certainty that if Albert really was dead, then he would want this to happen, would want the two people he loved most in the world to find solace and comfort in each other's arms, and that if he really was alive, he would want this to happen, for the very same reason... *Oh, Albert! Oh, Stefan! The loves of my life!*

I also knew – again with utter certainty – that Stefan was thinking and feeling exactly the same because there was such tenderness, such rawness and such a special sensitivity in his touch and in his movements, something that had never been there before. Something mystical and magical, something that had to do with this special moment in time. Some special passion mixed with this terrible sadness, which was mixed with tenderness, which was mixed with a knowingness that this was... yes... *this is... our life, our journey, our meeting and no one else could or should or would understand it... because it is ours and ours alone. Precious in a way that only we can understand... precious and ours... precious and ours...* so I let myself melt into his body, melt into his strength, melt into his passion and love and desire for me as he rhythmically and deliberately gained speed and momentum, seeking ever deeper into my depths as I opened ever wider to his power, until both of us were awash with life and infinite passion; swept away by the wonder of our coming together into a joining that was... aaahhhh....ooohhhh... incredibly bittersweet...and yes there it was...the incredible, bitter sweetness of us as we exploded into the darkness of that bittersweet night.

So there it was. Stefan and I were together again. And even if it was the same, the same tenderness and love between us, it was radically different. Because both of us were sad, grieving, lost, in shock.

It was as if we were stuck in the middle of a nightmare and couldn't find our way out.

There wasn't a whole lot to say or do, because we didn't know if Albert was dead or alive. After that call from Jacques Durand, we didn't hear anything more. No word, no news, and nobody knew what that meant. Was it a good sign or was it a sign that it was all over – that Albert was no longer in this world? That my beloved Albert, Stefan's beloved Albert, was really and truly gone? Neither one of us could bear to contemplate the thought, so we skirted around it, afraid that if we touched it, it might come true.

But the thought was always there.

Where was Albert?

Was he still alive?

And if so, what was happening to him?

What…

It simply didn't bear thinking about, and yet it was always there, always in our thoughts. How could it not be, however hard we tried to distract ourselves… however hard…

So we played ferociously with Daniel and Isabella and went for long walks on the footpath around Cap Ferrat, and then we would sit in silence on a rock or bench somewhere and gaze out at the sea while the children played. The weather was warm and beautiful and there were tourists everywhere, but we hardly noticed it. If we did, we'd go for a swim in the sea and swim frantically as if we thought we could drown our sorrow… but we couldn't, and the words – the dreadful words – *do you think Albert is dead?* – never passed our lips. They were just too painful.

And our lovemaking was the same.

It was frantic and ferocious and intense and sorrowful.

It was tender and passionate and silent and sad.

It was all things to us; both magical and mad.

But it couldn't make the pain go away.

And then there was the small matter of Stefan's wife, Monique, who was in Amsterdam with his daughters visiting family and friends there.

I broached the subject one evening after we'd put my kids to bed.

"Stefan," I said slowly, "does Monique know about us?"

There was a long silence; we were sitting on one of the big

white sofas in the lounge. The evening was quiet and still, not a wind was stirring outside.

"No," he said in typical Stefan fashion. He wasn't a talker.

"Oh," I said and sighed. "She's been so supportive of me throughout this whole ordeal…" I tried to continue, but the sentence just sort of ended in space. I wanted to say I had grown really fond of her, but didn't.

There was silence again.

"When is she coming back?"

"Not sure yet," he said, "but probably in a week or two. The girls are really having a good time up there seeing all their old friends…"

Another silence.

"She wanted me to fly up to Amsterdam and be with them for a few days, but when I told her about the call from the Foreign Ministry; she didn't press the matter."

His arm was around me now and feeling me shudder when he mentioned that call, he tightened his grip on me and buried his head in my neck, kissing me ever so softly.

I sighed and felt myself relaxing and melting into him as he began caressing me and touching me.

Then once again we were ravenously making love. Once again.

Kissing, touching and holding each other greedily and hungrily as if it was the only thing in the entire universe that could blot out our pain.

I felt myself slipping away, surrendering to the raw physicality of us.

So naked we lay there, and naked we joined, and naked we came once again.

Sex had become an obsession; our drug. The only way we could escape the pain.

And I had become addicted to it. And so had Stefan.

Addicted to sex.

And he liked it – and so did I.

Because for a moment there, in the sheer ecstasy of it, we managed to blot out the pain, the pain of not knowing how to deal with what could turn out to be the biggest loss either of us had ever experienced.

So there it was when I made love to Stefan. I knew it in my heart... I knew and understood that I had gone to a space beyond good pussy bad pussy... gone to a space beyond... because...

Real Love is unconditional.

Real Love is beyond borders.

Real Love is beyond names.

Real Love is Universal, all embracing, free.

Real Love is free flowing. Free flowing love.

Real Love is liberation.

Liberation from bondage.

Liberation from the prison of ideas.

Liberation from pain.

Liberation. Into the flow of Life.

Feeling the free-flowing Life Force.

Love!

And there I was, feeling it again.

Feeling the Love coursing through my veins... in and through me!

Alive! Moving! Breathing! Alive!

No ownership, no yours or mine, no this or that.

Just free and unlimited, free and unlimited Bliss.

Beyond the cage of words, beyond limitation, beyond good or bad.

Beyond you belong to me and I belong to you.

Beyond good pussy bad pussy... beyond...

A Divine Knowing, a Divine Certainty...

That this is Love... Love! Unconditional Love!

The free flowing of Life.
The free expression of Life.
The free movement of it in and through me.
The bliss of that, the joy of that, the present moment awareness of that…
LOVE!
FREEDOM!
FREE!

Even if only for a little while…

Later that night when we were completely done, exhausted, Stefan said to me, "I just don't know what to do, Rachel… I simply don't know what to do."

I knew exactly what he was talking about. He was talking about Monique. He was telling me that he couldn't tell Monique about him and me because they were working so hard to build up their very shaky marriage again.

"I know how much your family means to you," I said softly, holding him tightly in my arms, "… so don't think I don't under-stand."

I often wondered if Monique knew how many women Stefan had been with during their on-and-off marriage. Probably not. Maybe she didn't know anything… but that couldn't be the case because she was smart, really smart, and pretty streetwise… so of course she knew or guessed, at least some of it. But probably she was wise enough to let things lie.

"Maybe I can still see you a little when she gets back…" I said softly. The thought of losing him too was almost more than I could bear. I felt the tears coming.

"Yeah, maybe," he said, "but it will be difficult. Victor has quite a few business trips lined up for me in the next few months."

"Really?" I said in surprise. "Doing what?"

"Well, he says several of our major business partners in the region need reassuring since Albert's abduction and he wants me to go and talk to them personally. And this kind of visit can take two or three days for each one – you know, with the dinners and the ceremonial visits to their families and all. So Monique's not going to be happy with me being away so much."

"Oh, I see," I said. "Does it have to be you? Couldn't he send someone else?"

"That's what I said too, but he seems to think people will be most reassured if I come in person because almost everyone knows how close Albert and I have always been. He says they'll trust me when I tell them that business operations are continuing as usual – and will continue as usual – regardless of what...." And there his words died out...

He got up and started pacing the room.

"Damn, damn, damn!" he muttered. "Damn it to hell!"

A week later, right after Monique returned from Amsterdam with the girls, Victor called me down to the annex to tell me that he was hopeful that we would soon have real negotiations going on with Albert's kidnappers again.

"What?" I cried with joy when he told me. "Why haven't I heard? What did Jacques say?"

"Well, Rachel, you haven't heard this from Jacques because this time it's not through the Foreign Ministry," Victor said slowly, "it's through other channels... private channels."

"Oh... What do you mean?"

"Well, remember Albert's friend the Saudi Prince? Prince Abdul who was in Jordan with him?"

"Yes, of course."

"Well, it's through him."

"Really?" I said, my heart fluttering in my chest. "So the Foreign Ministry doesn't know about this?"

"That's right, and the Prince wants us to keep it that way."

"Oh, I see..." I said, trying to digest what he was saying.

"Why doesn't he want the Foreign Ministry to know? Victor! Can't you tell me more? Please!"

"No, I'm afraid I can't. I am just following the Prince's instructions. So all I can tell you at the moment is that the Prince is hopeful. He told me his people are now in contact with a group in Yemen claiming to know the whereabouts of Albert... which is a good sign... but it's a very delicate situation, which is why he doesn't want us speaking to anyone about it. Do you understand what I'm saying, Rachel?"

I felt myself trembling all over. *Oh, Albert! Maybe he is still alive...*

When I didn't reply, Victor continued slowly, "Look Rachel, I don't want you to get your hopes up too much. This is a hopeful sign... but..."

Then the phone rang, interrupting us.

He picked it up and spoke a few words in German. Then he covered the mouthpiece and said to me, "Sorry, Rachel, but this is an important call. I'll keep you posted."

I turned and walked slowly out of the annex... as if in a dream, shaking all over....

Oh, tender bird of hope!

A few days later, Victor called me again from the annex while Isabella was taking her afternoon nap and asked me to come down and talk to him.

My heart skipped a beat.

"Do you have news about Albert?" I cried.

"Rachel, you know I don't like talking about these things on the phone. So just come down to my office, will you?"

"Okay, okay, I'll be right there."

I dropped everything and told Amélie to look after Isabella. Then I rushed out the door and ran down to the annex at the end of the property. *Does he have news about Albert?*

The door was open, so I went barging in.

Victor was standing in the middle of the room, which was unusual. Usually he was at his desk. Something didn't seem right.

"Has something happened to Albert?" I cried. "Do you know something?"

"No, no, no, Rachel.Now just come in and let's sit down." He closed the door behind me.

"But what's going on, Victor?" I cried.

"Now just take it easy, will you. I don't have any news about Albert... None whatsoever. I swear... Now come and sit down with me."

He led me over to the couch. "Coffee?" he asked as he picked up the pot of coffee.

"No, thank you," I replied, confused by his manner. "What's going on?"

"Will you just sit down and relax, Rachel," he said again. "I want to talk to you."

"Oh," I said and sat down next to him.

He poured himself a cup of coffee and kept me waiting.

"Well, what do you want to talk about, Victor?" I said finally, feeling flustered and confused.

"Rachel," he said slowly, clearing his throat, "I've been thinking about your situation here now that Albert has been missing for so long... "

"What about my situation?" I asked.

"Well, you know that legally you have no rights here. You have no right to Albert's money or even to be here, living in his house. In fact, you're only here because I have allowed you to be here and because I have continued to fund your stay here with your children."

I stiffened all over when I heard his words.

"What?" I cried in surprise, "What are you talking about?"

"What I am saying, Rachel, is that your situation is rather precarious because since you are not Albert's wife, you have no legal claim to anything of Albert's. That's all I'm saying, and I'm also saying that the reality is you've been able to stay here basically thanks to me."

"What?" I jumped up, "What are you talking about Victor! Have you lost your mind? Albert loves me and we have a child together. Isabella is his daughter!"

Then I just stood there with my hands on my hips, glaring at him, thinking the man had really lost it.

"Now, now, now, Rachel," he replied slowly, stirring his coffee, "there's no need to get so upset. Why don't you just sit down and take it easy." He spoke as if he'd been expecting me to react like this and was prepared. "I was just pointing out the reality of your situation to you. The reality of your legal situation, I mean, and the fact that you are still here in his house – living the good life – thanks to me."

I was so shocked and furious that I turned and made for the door, my heart pounding in my chest.

He jumped up after me and grabbed my arm saying, "Not so hasty, Rachel. Please come and sit down and talk to me. I am sure we can work something out."

"But I don't want to talk to you," I cried. "Let me go!"

But he didn't. "I don't think that's a good idea, Rachel," he said, still holding my arm. "In fact, I'm quite sure it wouldn't be a good idea."

The way he said those words sent chills up and down my spine. Suddenly I had this sinking feeling in my stomach. Something bad was about to go down, I was sure.

"Now let's go back to the couch and sit down. I have a proposal for you. You see, I know you've been sleeping with Stefan."

"Bastard!" I cried, pulling my arm free and heading for the door.

"Just one more thing, Rachel, before you leave: I suggest you ask yourself, my dear… If you don't cooperate with me, who's going to pay the five million Euros ransom for Albert's freedom if I don't? Is there anyone else you know besides me who has access to the company's money?"

His words made me stop cold in my tracks.

I turned and looked at him in disbelief.

"What?" I cried.

He didn't answer.

"Would you really…"

"Yes, Rachel… I would… really… now come back here and sit down beside me."

When he said those words, it was as if he'd punched me in the stomach, and I knew I was beaten.

I just stood there dumbstruck, loathing the man.

When I didn't move, he came over to me and took my arm again, but now all the fight had gone out of me. He led me docilely back to the couch. I sat down without a word; I knew what was coming.

He put his left arm around me and slowly pushed the hair back from my face with his right hand. I felt the hot tears in my eyes began to trickle slowly down my cheeks.

Even though I was crying, his hand moved down my face and along my neck until it rested softly on my left breast. I closed my eyes, hating the man.

"Rachel," he said, breathing more heavily now, "I've wanted you for so long."

"But I don't want you!" I hissed fiercely, pushing his hand away. "In fact, I hate you! Hate you! Can't you see that?"

"Ah, but Rachel, I know that doesn't matter so much to you! Indeed, not that much at all. You see, I know you slept with Felix Fischer – not because you wanted to… but because Albert wanted you to." I felt myself stiffen.

"But that was then!" I cried heatedly. "That was a long time ago. Things have changed since then."

"Changed?" He began caressing my breast again, fondling my

nipple and then holding it tight between his fingers, pulling the nipple out.

I tried to push him away but he was stronger than I expected.

"Changed?" he repeated again, still pinching my nipple. "I don't think so. You see, I've known that rake Albert for many more years than you have. I've seen the women come and go. You're no different than the rest, my little lady – just in case you think you are."

I pushed his hand away again and struggled to free myself from his grip, "But it's not true. Albert loves me and asked me to marry him!"

At that Victor laughed heartily. "Oh, he did, did he? So how come no one knows about it except you?"

I managed to free myself from his tight hold on me and jumped up from the couch.

"Because he asked me the night before he left for Jordan," I replied hotly, loathing the man.

"And you expect me to believe that?" said Victor, still sitting on the couch. He was laughing again. "Oh, you women, you're all the same. All wanting to get your claws into the man with the good looks and the money."

He pressed a control button on the side table and the curtains were silently and swiftly drawn in all the windows. Now the room was in semi-darkness.

It was very quiet.

"Now come and sit down, Rachel," he said slowly. When I didn't he added, "If you want to see Albert again, you'd better do exactly as I say. Now come and sit down and unbutton your blouse, so I can touch you."

"But how can you do this, Victor?" I cried desperately. "How can you?"

"Just come and sit down, Rachel, and unbutton your blouse."

I felt hot and cold all over; I simply didn't know what to do.

"Did you hear me, Rachel... did you?"

I did hear him, so I walked slowly back over to the couch again and sat down meekly.

I couldn't look at him.

"I hate you!" I hissed under my breath. "I hate you!"

"Now unbutton your blouse…"

"How can you do this to me? How can you…"

I felt his hot breath on my neck as he whispered in my ear, "Because I want you… Now, Rachel… unbutton your blouse…"

Tears of rage were trickling down my face as I slowly did what he said. When my blouse was unbuttoned, he pushed it back towards my shoulders and felt my breasts for a moment through my beautiful blue lace bra.

"But I don't want you…" I cried. "I don't…"

He undid my bra.

Seeing my breasts suddenly free like that excited him so much that he sighed with pleasure. When he let go of me to move from the couch to the floor in front of me, I tried to get up again but this time, he pushed me forcefully back onto the couch.

"Now… now Rachel…"

He was stronger than I expected.

Then he leaned forward and began kissing my bare breasts, holding them and fondling them.

"You bastard!" I cried, struggling to free myself but he wouldn't let me go.

Instead, he stopped and took a hold of my shoulders vehemently and regarded me with his mean, lustful eyes. "Did you understand what I just said to you, Rachel? Did you? Or do I need to explain it to you once more. Who's going to pay the ransom for Albert's release if you don't cooperate with me? Tell me who…"

When I didn't answer, he took my face in his hands and began to kiss me on the mouth. I was so appalled at what was happening that my mouth was shut tight like a clam.

"Come, come, my dear, this won't do at all…"

His hands sought my breasts again and he began fondling and pinching my nipples.

And then, as the grim reality of what was going down really began to dawn of me, I shuddered inside because I knew what it meant. I knew it meant that not only did I have to let him fuck me, but that I had to do more than just let him…. I had to….

The realization only made the tears flow even more freely down my wet cheeks as he kissed me again and again. Mouth to mouth. I forced myself to open my mouth a little and immediately felt his tongue seeking me out. Boring down on me, into me.

All I could think of was how God-awful it was, how God-awful awful… that this wonderful, beautiful thing called sex could become so debased. Could be used against me, against Albert, against our love. But I knew I had to do it. I knew I had to for Albert – to make sure Victor paid the ransom, to make sure Albert came back to me alive, to make sure…

He was breathing heavily now and unbuttoning my jeans, trying to get his hands inside them. But they were too tight.

"Take them off," he said hoarsely, suddenly there was urgency in his voice. "Hurry up."

I shimmied them slowly down over my hips and took them off as he stood up, unbuttoning his shirt and taking off his trousers. Now all I had on were my panties, the beautiful, blue lace ones Albert had given me, the ones I loved so much and he loved so much. Victor's fingers were now inside those beautiful panties, finding my pussy, touching her, caressing her. But she wasn't happy or wet or ready for this; she was closed tight in defiance.

Discovering how dry she was, he removed his fingers.

"Lie back," he said, pushing me back on the couch. Then he removed my panties and slid down and began licking my pussy, trying to make her very wet. But he was in too much of a hurry and instead fished a tube of lube out of his pants pocket; his need was that great. He'd wanted me for so long and now I was there, naked, open and vulnerable – within his grasp. So he squeezed some lube out of the tube and when he thought my pussy was wet enough, he hurriedly stood up and took off his briefs. His manhood was erect, pulsing, wanting me, wanting my pussy and in one fell swoop he came down on me, pushing me back on the couch, entering me and burying himself deep in me. He was not a gentle man, nor a man who knew how to make a woman's body sing – rather he was driven by his own need, and so he took me in a fury, hard and fast, crying out my name and coming almost before I had time to adjust to his hardness in me.

But he didn't care and neither did I.

Because we both knew, each in our own way, that there would be more, much, much more…. which meant I would have plenty of time, oh yes, plenty of time, to adjust to his needs and desires, and plenty of time to please him in exactly the way he wanted to be pleased.

After that, there wasn't much I could do.

Now that Victor had blackmailed me so effectively, I knew there would be no stopping him. He'd found a way to trap me and he was going to use it to the fullest. I was caught like a fly in a spider's web. There was no way out. The man was obsessed with me and had obviously been so for a long time. So I knew I could expect no mercy.

The next morning, he called me to tell me of his plans. It seemed he'd given the matter much thought.

"Rachel," he said, "I want you to come down to the annex in the afternoon while Daniel is at playschool and Isabella is taking her nap just as we have been doing. I don't want to arouse anyone's suspicions; I want it to look like business as usual. So just tell Amélie to look after Isabella while you're gone, and tell her we are not to be disturbed even if Isabella wakes up. Say we're in the middle of some very delicate talks with Albert's captors and the Foreign Ministry, and we mustn't be disturbed under any circumstances. Tell her she's to take care of Isabella until you come back."

My heart sank when I heard his words.

"I'll instruct Madam Raffin to keep any guests away," he went on, sounding very buoyant, "and I'll tell her the same – that we're in the middle of delicate talks and don't want to be disturbed no matter what. You must tell this to everyone you talk to, do you understand? Everyone including Stefan."

There was a pause; then he added, "One last thing, Rachel. Don't even think about telling Stefan. Because if you do, I'll go straight to Monique and tell her Stefan has been sleeping with you again.AGAIN! Do you understand? Again! That would most definitely mean the end of their marriage, which I'm quite sure Stefan wouldn't appreciate at all."

When I didn't reply, he said, "Rachel, are you listening?"

"Yes," I replied slowly, "I am Victor... but I just don't understand how you can..."

He cut me off before I could finish.

"Rachel, do you remember what I said about the ransom money?"

When I didn't reply, he added slowly. "In case, you don't remember, I said if you didn't cooperate, who knows what could happen to Albert." Then he hung up.

For a long time, I sat there, staring at the phone, thinking, *what can I do? What?*

Is there anyone who can help me?

Anyone I can tell?

Anyone?

I couldn't think of anyone.

Besides my mother, Albert and Stefan, no one would believe me if I told them that Victor Gandler, Albert's CEO, was blackmailing me. No one would believe that Albert's closest business ally would refuse to pay the ransom for his release if I didn't oblige him with the sexual favors he demanded. It was too tall a tale. Everyone I knew in the south of France was either a friend or business associate of Albert and Victor. A tale like that would just make them laugh. Who was I anyway? Just a newcomer, the new kid on the block. Most of them probably regarded me in the same way as Victor did – as just another one of Albert's many women. Albert and I hadn't been there long enough for any of these people to really get to know me. It would have been one thing if it was public knowledge that Albert wanted to marry me – if he had announced it to the world and we were engaged. But the way things stood, no one would believe me if I told them that Albert had proposed to me the night before he left for Jordan. They'd all laugh like Victor did and think it was just some story I made up.

What a mess!

I was trapped. Trapped!

I picked up my phone to call Stefan; he was my only hope, regardless of what Victor said. But then I remembered that Victor had sent Stefan off on an extended trip to Cairo and Beirut and Amman that very morning to meet and reassure some of their important business associates just as Stefan said he would.

Damn! Was that really the reason Victor sent Stefan off that very morning? Or was it just because he wanted to be sure Stefan wasn't around when he sprung his little trap? He knew Stefan was the only ally I had on Cap Ferrat.

Oh that conniving bastard! Of all the mean and evil…

My blood was boiling.

Of course that's why he sent Stefan off to all those places! Victor wanted to make sure he wouldn't have to deal with Stefan if I turned to him for help and protection.

Damn him to hell!

I was furious, furious because I knew I was trapped.

I shuddered to think what was coming.

I picked up my phone to call my mother. But how could I call her? She was in hospital at the moment, suffering from the strain of taking care of my sister Marlene. But what if I did call her? What would she say? Would she say it was more important for me to flee from this madman, even if it meant that Albert would die? No, of course she wouldn't say that. She was a woman of the world who had slept with many men, just like me.

Then I thought about calling the police. But what good would that do? It would still come down to Victor's word against mine. No one would believe me. I had no proof. Everyone would believe Victor, Albert's trusted CEO. They'd just look upon me as another gold digger who was trying to get her tenterhooks into Albert and his fortune.

Ugh!

I shuddered and put down my phone. No, there was no reason to call my mother or the police. I knew what I had to do. I had to save the man I loved... the man I loved with all my heart... the man who was being held captive by madmen in the Middle East...

If fucking Victor Gandler was the only way to do it, then I had to do it...

Suddenly I couldn't help but laugh at the irony of it all... because it dawned on me that Albert wasn't the only one being held captive by madmen. Now I too was being held captive by a madman...

That afternoon when I went down to the annex, Victor was ravenous. Hungry. Insatiable.

All he wanted to do was touch me all over and kiss my nipples and pussy and then penetrate me. He was afire. Now that he had me trapped, he wasn't going to waste any time getting what he wanted. As soon as Madam Raffin had served our tea and left, he came over to the couch where I was sitting and pressed the button on the side table so the curtains were drawn in all the windows.

With Madam Raffin gone, he didn't have to pretend anymore. He pulled up the ottoman and sat down in front of me, surveying me as if I was his prey.

He leaned towards me and said hoarsely, "Take off your t-shirt and your jeans, Rachel; I want to look at you."

When I didn't move immediately, he looked displeased.

"Victor," I said softly, "can't we just talk for a moment."

"Talk?" he laughed. "What is there to talk about?"

"What about Albert?" I tried to say calmly, but there was hysteria in my voice, "Don't you care about him?"

That didn't please him at all, in fact, my words made him furious.

He leaned forward and grabbed me by the shoulders. "Rachel, I am warning you! Don't push me or you'll never see Albert again!"

I was surprised by his vehemence.

"Now take off your t-shirt and jeans."

I did what he said. Suddenly I was afraid. The man had really gone mad.

When my t-shirt and jeans were off, he threw them over in the corner and sat back down on the ottoman before me.

"Now take off your bra and give it to me."

When it was off, he took it and examined the fine lace carefully. Then he tossed it over in the corner with my other clothes.

He sat there gazing at me for a while and then he said, "Now hold your breasts and lift them towards me."

When I did that, he said, "Aaaahh… Nice, very nice. Now take off your panties and spread your legs so I can see you."

I started to shimmy my panties down.

"And do it slowly…"

I did as he said.

"Slowly…"

When my panties were off, he started unbuttoning his shirt.

"Now spread your legs."

He stood up, and with his eyes riveted on me he took off his shoes, shirt, pants and briefs. His penis was already erect and pulsing. He got down on the floor before me and took hold of my knees and spread my legs open as wide as he could. Then he bent forward and began hungrily kissing and licking my inner thighs, working his way up to my pussy.

I heard him moan.

Even if I was tense and closed tight, I knew I couldn't win. I remembered his chilling words about cooperating.

When he reached my pussy, he started kissing her, making her very wet and ready. After that, he opened her with his fingers and pulled back, looking at her as if he was inspecting an incredible treasure he had just discovered.

Then he caressed her again and kissed her, sucking on her tender lips.

When he was sure I was wet enough, he crawled up to me to kiss me on the mouth. As he did so, his hands found my nipples.

So far I had just been lying there, passive, unmoved.

"Remember what I said about cooperating, Rachel?" he said hoarsely.

He pinched my nipples hard.

"Do you?" he said, squeezing them tightly between his fingers. "Do you?"

I moaned even if I didn't want to.

"Now that's better."

He kept holding my nipples, squeezing them tightly and twisting them until I was moaning with pain and pleasure.

"So you like it rough, do you?"

He held my nipples tightly, hurting me and pleasing me against my will.

I moaned again.

Hearing me moan like that excited him even more; so much so that he could no longer wait. He entered me and I felt his penis growing inside me, seeking my depths. He was still clutching my nipples, holding them and pinching them, while he thrust himself deeper and deeper into me. And even though I hated the man, there was something about the way he held my nipples that made my pussy catch fire.

Good pussy bad pussy! Oh no!

That was when I heard myself starting to moan and felt my hips swaying, mirroring and catching his fire and his rhythm, even though I didn't want to and hated the man. But there he was, bearing down on me, holding me down, bending me to his will, forcing me to submit. And even if my mind was screaming *NO! NO! NO,* the man was deep inside me and good pussy bad pussy was being swept away in the raging tide of his all-consuming lust.

Suddenly he was coming and coming hard, and to my great surprise, good pussy bad pussy was too... coming and coming hard with him.

Victor was very pleased with me. Very pleased indeed.

So he lusted after me continually.

And almost every day, almost every afternoon, he availed himself of my beautiful, innocent body.

And I let him.

PART II

ALBERT'S STORY

A sea change took place in the heart of Albert Giovanni when he met Rachel Somers that summer, two years earlier, in Nice. No one would have expected it to happen, least of all, Albert himself.

He was a man in his prime, forty-eight years old, rich and good-looking with scores of women after him. He was cocksure, worldly and used to getting his way.

But then he met Rachel Somers and everything changed.

It all started that warm balmy evening in late August when Stefan brought Rachel to dinner at Chez Paul. Albert, who was a little bored with life, wasn't expecting much to happen that evening. It was the twenty-fourth of August.

Sometimes Albert and Stefan shared the women Stefan hooked up with – just for the fun of it. It had been their way for a long, long time.

The two of them – that is Albert and Stefan – went way back. In fact, all the way back to Stefan's early student days in Vienna when he worked in Albert's father's offices. Right from the beginning, Stefan, with his astonishing blond, good looks, had been a magnet for women. But coming down from a little village in the mountains of Austria as he did, he was a total innocent – and all that female attention just bewildered him. So Albert took pity on the young man and took him under his wing, becoming his friend and mentor. The wise older brother who adroitly taught Stefan how to navigate in the traitorous waters of women. It wasn't difficult for Albert to do because Albert, with his aristocratic charm and dark, fiery eyes, was quite a magnet for women in his own right. So that was how it all began... their friendship and the way they shared women. It just happened naturally and continued right up until that evening at Chez Paul when Rachel

Somers walked into Albert Giovanni's life.

Stefan and Rachel were already at the table when Albert arrived.

"Ah, so this is Rachel," he said, as she stood up to greet him. "Please, please sit down. Stefan has told me about you. I hope you are enjoying your stay here."

He touched her luxurious chestnut hair softly as she sat down.

Where does Stefan find them? He wondered to himself. *This one is really stunning.*

Once they were seated, Albert acted as if he barely noticed Rachel, but he did. *What a beauty,* he thought smiling inwardly. She actually surpassed most of the women Stefan hooked up with, whenever his down-to-earth, Dutch wife, Monique, threw him out of their very on-and-off marriage.

Albert started talking business with Stefan in German.

But then he stopped when he realized Rachel was quietly regarding him with those amazing, green eyes of hers. "Just a little business, my dear, I am sure you understand."

What eyes she has!

At that moment, Albert decided he would take advantage of this opportunity to indulge himself with yet another one of the women Stefan brought into his life. *Life is boring enough,* he thought. *This one might be interesting.*

His promiscuous lifestyle was not something he ever questioned; it was just the way it was. After meditating for years in a remote monastery in Japan when he was a young man, there was very little that could ruffle him. When a woman caught his eye, he would go after her – for no other reason than to please himself. He never considered the consequences.

Albert took a thin white envelope out of his jacket pocket and gave it to Stefan. "Please give Mr. Hadid my apologies for being unable to meet him tonight. Make some excuse about me being called away suddenly and give him this."

Stefan took the envelope and understood he wouldn't be

leaving the dinner table with Rachel, Albert would. "It's a personal invitation to Hadid to come to the house on Cap Ferrat with his wife. You know how important he is to our new set-up in Egypt."

When dinner was over, he sent Stefan off and took Rachel back to his condo in Nice with its spectacular view of the coast to indulge himself. It was a lovely evening. A gentle breeze came in from the sea and one could hear the soft night noises of people down below on their way to various pleasures and boredom.

Rachel stood on the balcony with its incredible sea view. The stars were shining brightly and Albert thought she looked so small and forlorn standing there. Like a little lost bird.

"Come inside," he said.

He put on some quiet music and took Rachel in his arms, dancing slowly as he regarded her.

"Why did you leave your husband for Stefan?"

Rachel looked at him with those big green eyes of hers and considered his question. "Oh, I don't know... I just couldn't help myself."

"Ahh..." he said, "so the blood in your veins runs very hot, is that it?"

He took her chin and lifted it up towards him, examining her lovely face. She seemed shy and unsure of herself. There was just something about her. A purity... an innocence... He felt himself becoming aroused even though he hadn't touched her yet.

"Let's see if you really are as warm as you are beautiful," he said, leading her over to one of the few armchairs in the sparsely furnished, spacious living room.

Once she was sitting, he positioned himself on the floor before her and began kissing her on the mouth. She didn't resist, nor did she participate. Then he began fondling her nipples through the low-cut, creamy white dress she was wearing. He had the strange feeling she was regarding him from afar... watching and waiting...

He already knew she had no panties on. That was part of his arrangement with Stefan. *I prefer my women with no panties on...* he always said... *it makes it easier... to get what I want...*

He took hold of her legs and placed them on the arms of the chair so she was open to him, spread eagle; then he went down on her. Open as she was, she didn't resist. It was as if she was still waiting, watching, testing the water, until all of a sudden her body language changed and told him now she wanted more of his tongue caressing her pussy. He knew what women liked; he had that power.

Her hips moved.

She's not as innocent as she looks...

Desire flared in him, a sudden beacon in the night. Now he wanted to control her, wanted her to want him... wanted to see her do his bidding... wanted to make her come...

"You're... you're," she mumbled, suddenly awash with shy emotion and passion.

"I want to see you come," he murmured in her ear. Now he was the spectator, the one in control. He continued caressing her gently, with all his knowingness as he bent her to his will, not suspecting that he was unleashing forces which were more powerful than he was and way beyond his control.

"Aahhh..." she cried, hips swaying as she came to a shuddering climax. She was beautiful in her innocence, opening to him. So beautiful that now he wanted her too.

He pulled her up from the chair, giving her no time to recover. "Take off your dress."

He was surprised she didn't protest but did exactly as he said, without a word...

*Look at her...*It took his breath away. *She's...!!*

He led her to the low bed in the bedroom – and there he fucked her, coming hard and fast. But when they were done, to his own great and eternal surprise, he turned to her again. And slowly and gently made real love to her. Real, true, gentle love...

because something was happening he wasn't expecting, something was happening he wasn't prepared for; a sea change was taking place and sweeping through his heart. There was no denying it.

The earth had moved for Albert Giovanni when he looked into the eyes of this green-eyed beauty and he experienced a true joining, maybe for the first time in his entire life. A true joining, a mind-boggling joining. He felt it and so did she...

The second time he saw her, it was the same. It was as if he was sucked into a maelstrom, his emotions were that strong. And it took him by surprise. Again.

It was at a party he was giving at his house on Cap Ferrat shortly after. It was an all-day affair for his business connections and the team around him. Stefan, of course, was invited and he brought Rachel. Albert found her by the pool chatting with Joey and Carl, while Stefan was off talking to Michelle about the recent incident in Beirut. He came up behind her and put his hands on her shoulders. It was as if an electric shock ran through his body the moment he touched her.

She turned around, fixing her green eyes upon him in a soft, solemn gaze.

He exchanged a few words with Joey and Carl and then he took her hand and said, "Come, let me show you my house."

He led her up towards the big house on the hill. On the way, they met Felix Fischer, a big, bear-like man who was sweating profusely in the warm, mid-September afternoon sun. The two conversed for a moment in German and then suddenly Fischer stopped in mid-sentence and stared at Rachel.

"Rachel, this is Felix Fischer from Hamburg. I am doing a little business with him. Would you be kind enough to give him your hand? He doesn't speak English but he seems to be quite taken with you..."

She shook hands with him and then Albert led her up to his

house.

They ended up in his spacious office with its minimalist design on the lower floor of the house. The room had a breathtaking view of the Mediterranean. Suddenly alone with Albert again, Rachel seemed shy and unsure of herself. Albert felt slightly uneasy too – so taken aback was he by his own feelings.

What's happening to me? he thought. He wanted to take her in his arms and smother her with kisses right away, but he didn't. Instead he brushed her hair away from her face and said, "Come, my dear, don't be so serious. It's not good for you."

Music for Zen Meditation by Tony Scott was playing in the background. The sounds harmonized perfectly with the stark, minimalist atmosphere of the room.

"What do you mean?" Rachel replied softly.

"You're wearing yourself out for no good reason. You're thinking and worrying all the time and it's exhausting you. Always trying to figure things out, trying to deduct what's going on, speculating, worrying. You're probably worrying about your son right now, tormenting yourself because you ran off to have your little fling with Stefan."

When she didn't reply, he beckoned her to sit down on the couch with him.

Albert broke the soft silence that enveloped them by telling her a little about his years of study and meditation in the Far East. "One of the main things I learned," he said, "was that it's vitally important to focus your energy on the situation at hand instead of dissipating your strength and power by worrying about things you can do nothing about."

Rachel listened quietly, fixing her solemn gaze on him once again. It startled him, the way she looked at him. He actually felt she was present, really there.

"Albert, why are you telling me all this?" she asked innocently.

He gazed into space, surprised at how well she read him.

"I should have met you before you married and had a son."

"What do they have to do with it, now that I've left them?" she replied slowly.

"Ah, but you'll go back to them and probably soon… but until you do…" he moved closer to her, "let's see what happens…" He started kissing her hungrily on the mouth while his hand moved slowly up her leg. Suddenly the door to his office swung open. It was Stefan. He seemed surprised to see Rachel and Albert like that – and not especially pleased.

"I was looking for Rachel," was all he said.

Albert stood up.

They exchanged words in German. Rachel got up, ready to go with Stefan.

Albert turned and motioned her to sit down. "It seems Stefan forgot something important he must attend to."

Stefan slammed the door and left without looking back.

Albert laughed and locked the door.

"Well, Rachel, now you know how Stefan feels about you."

"I'd really like to go with Stefan," she said out of loyalty to Stefan, but he didn't believe her. He knew the force field between them was too powerful; he was sure she felt it too.

He drew the curtains.

"Now stand up and take off your dress," he said.

She didn't protest but stood up and looked at him. "Do you really want me that much?" The way she said it made him tremble inside.

"Isn't that obvious, Rachel?" Now he'd spoken, now he'd said it. Confessed – and his heart swelled as he bore down upon her.

The voice within him was saying *I want her to be mine. Mine!* He didn't know where that voice was coming from, but he was sure he heard it. And it was plain as day.

A few days later, Albert found himself at dinner with Felix Fischer. They were wrapping up their business dealings for the moment. But suddenly the burly German was asking him about the woman he bumped into with Albert at Albert's house party the other day.

"The green-eyed one," Felix said, laughing lewdly. "She's a beauty."

When Albert didn't reply, Felix went on.

"How about arranging a little, intimate tete-a-tete for me with her, before I go back to Germany, my friend?" Felix Fischer was not only vulgar and gross, he was also one of Giovanni International's biggest contractors in Germany. Albert and Felix had a long history of very good and profitable business relations, so Albert had often supplied him with beautiful women when Felix was in the south of France on business. It was just the way things were done. It had never bothered Albert before, but now Felix was talking about Rachel.

"You know... a little rendezvous," Felix repeated, thumping his bear-like hand on table. He'd had a bit too much to drink. "She has very nice tits... I am sure!" He laughed heartily.

Albert felt his stomach contract.

"And a nice pussy... you have tried her out, it seems," said Felix, guessing correctly.

So Albert ended up doing as he was wont to do; he arranged or rather manipulated Rachel into servicing Felix Fischer by threatening to send Stefan into exile in Beirut if she didn't. He knew it was a cruel, wretched thing to do, but he did it nevertheless. He wasn't ready to admit the depths of his feelings for her – not yet anyway.

But the night it actually happened, the night he so casually and ruthlessly handed Rachel over to Felix Fischer in his condo overlooking the Mediterranean, was a night he'd never forget. Albert was already there with Felix, having a drink, when Rachel and Stefan arrived. She looked so gorgeous and innocent that night – and absolutely terrified.

*What am I doing...*he thought when he looked at her, as she sat there frozen at Stefan's side while the three men laughed and talked in German. *Here is this angel, this perfect beauty of a woman and I'm throwing her to that beast.*

His mind was in turmoil.

He felt like a pervert, a madman, a maniac.

But it's too late to change my mind. I can't go back on my word.

The moment he and Stefan left Rachel alone with Felix, he felt his gut contract in pain. *What have I done?* his insides cried out. He couldn't even bear to be with Stefan – so he promptly sent him off on a late flight to Cairo.

He drove back to his house on Cap Ferrat and spent most of that long night pacing the floor of his office. He simply wasn't prepared for the way he felt. The whole thing was so unexpected; it had taken him completely by surprise.

Who is this woman?

Where did she come from?

He'd never felt anything like this before – not in his whole life. It was as if there was a high voltage charge between Rachel and him from the moment they met.

He shivered thinking of the first time he made love to her. He'd been with so many women before, so many he couldn't even remember all their names or faces, nor did he care to. He'd been a rich bon vivant all his life, a good-looking charmer, a man of wealth and power who could have any woman he pointed at. But with Rachel it was different from the get-go. He'd felt strangely drawn to her, strangely attracted… as if he already knew her…

Then he thought back to the day of his party, and how they'd accidently bumped into Felix on the way up to his house. He remembered the lecherous look on Felix's face; the man was so stunned by her beauty he almost salivated over her.

Damn, he thought. *Damn it to hell! It is true; she is a magnificent beauty. An unspoiled gem. And look what I've done.*

He simply couldn't explain it to himself. Couldn't explain

why he had manipulated Rachel – actually blackmailed her – into giving her innocent body to that despicable man. He cringed at the thought of it. At the thought of her, Rachel, and her soft, exquisite body in the arms of that coarse, vulgar oaf.

How could I?

Of course he told himself that he did it because that had been his way – to arrange for beautiful women to entertain his important business contacts. But this time it was different. This time it was Rachel! A woman who was different, a woman who he'd experienced something unforgettable with... so it didn't make any sense....

What was I thinking?

He couldn't stop pacing the floor.

His thoughts were driving him crazy.

By four in the morning, he could contain himself no longer, so he drove back to Nice to find her. First he went to the condo, but all he found there was Felix alone, passed out on the big bed with a bottle of Scotch beside him, snoring loudly. *The lout! Well, at least she's not here. But where is she?*

He went to the hotel where she was staying with Stefan, but the front desk said she wasn't in their suite either. So he walked the empty streets of Nice looking for her.

Where is she? Where can she be?

Finally, he found her sitting in a deserted café, staring into an empty coffee cup. She didn't see him. He stood in the open doorway, gazing at her.

Oh my God, what have I done?

She looked so little and forlorn sitting there; her riotous, chestnut hair falling carelessly around her lovely face, which was half-hidden from view.

He walked over to the table where she was sitting.

She looked up, obviously surprised to see him.

"I wanted to see if you were okay," he said quietly.

She regarded him guardedly.

"Yeah, I guess so."

"Come, let's get you out of here," he said pulling her up from the chair and taking her arm as if she was a wounded soldier. She was so wiped out she almost couldn't stand on her feet; so he supported her and steered her down the street to his waiting Porsche. Once he had her snuggled in the car, he drove fiercely back to his house on Cap Ferrat. He didn't say a word, nor did she. When they arrived, he took her up to his bedroom, undressed her and put her in his big bed. She was asleep before her head hit the pillow.

When she finally awoke in the middle of the next day, he brought her breakfast in bed and watched her eat. They still hadn't spoken.

At last, he said, "I'm sorry about last night. It was wrong of me…"

When she heard his words, she burst out crying.

"I should have known," he said, moving toward her. He wanted to hold her, comfort her, but he didn't dare. "I should have respected you for who you are, Rachel, from the beginning…"

His words only made her cry more.

His heart ached so when he saw her like that. *Oh my God, what have I done?* He wanted to touch her, but still he didn't dare.

Suddenly she stopped crying and looked at him and said, "Albert, I must know… was it liberation or bondage… what happened last night? Which was it… please, tell me! I must know!"

When he heard those words, he burst out laughing. "Oh, Rachel," he cried. "You are simply a miracle. A miracle! Where have you been all my life?" And with that he bent forward and took her face in his hands and hungrily kissed her lips.

Oh, Rachel!

She was so genuine, so authentic, so real. It was then, at that very moment, that Albert Giovanni knew beyond a shadow of a doubt that he loved Rachel Somers. The certainty of his feelings was so powerful that it almost overwhelmed him.

What is more, it continued, that certainty, for the next two days of absolute bliss they shared together at his house. Now that no one was there, they had the whole place, the house, the gardens, the pool, the sea below – everything – all to themselves. They were all alone. All alone to play and frolic and enjoy each other – and so they did. It was as if they had entered another time and space – a magic garden – that only they could enter. And there they lingered. Touching, tasting, kissing, merging into some greater whole, some larger beingness than either of them had experienced before. There was a tranquility in the air and in them, a knowingness, as if they'd known each other before, in another time, in another place, in another lifetime...

He was stretched out by the pool, watching her dangling her feet in the water, when the call came from Beirut and he had to fly off at a moment's notice.

"There's a business emergency," he said softly. "I have to go..."

She looked stunned, bereft.

"I'll call you when I get back," he said, and was gone.

But when he did get back, three days later, the world had changed. And changed drastically.

Albert had Stefan on the phone.

"What?"

"Yes," Stefan repeated slowly, "she's pregnant... Rachel's pregnant."

"What?"

Pregnant!

There was a long silence.

"You can't be serious."

"Yes, I'm afraid I am... and when I told her she'd have to have an abortion, she said she wouldn't." Stefan didn't sound happy at all.

Albert whistled softly through his teeth.

He knew Stefan wouldn't want another baby since he was having trouble enough trying to be a father to the two children he already had.

His mind was reeling. *Rachel... pregnant... pregnant with Stefan's baby? How could that be?*

"Is it your baby?" Albert finally asked.

"She says she's not sure... she says it could be me or her husband, Jan."

"Oh, I see..." said Albert, trying to process this new piece of information.

There was another long silence.

Then Albert cleared his throat and said, "Well, maybe I can talk some sense into her. She's got to have an abortion. Look, I have some business to attend first, but I'll come by as soon as I can and have a talk with her."

A few days later, Albert went to the hotel.

When Rachel came down to the lobby to meet him, the first thing he did was brush her lovely, riotous chestnut hair from her face and lift her chin towards him so he could look at her. She was as beautiful and thoughtful as ever.

His heart contracted. *Ah, Rachel!*

He didn't say a word, nor did she. Instead, he took her by the hand and led her to his car and drove to a secluded spot along the coast. He pulled over and turned off the engine. The sky was so very blue that day.

He kissed her passionately on the mouth.

She returned his kiss, just as passionately.

She loves me. He felt the thrill of it resounding through him.

"Rachel, darling, you can't be serious about not having an abortion."

"So Stefan told you I was pregnant."

"Yes, he did."

There was a long silence.

Then she took Albert's hand and said very slowly, "But I am serious."

"But what will you do with a baby? There's no future for you here with a baby, you must see that."

"Yes, I do." She looked as if she was going to cry, but she didn't.

"But Rachel, we were doing so nicely... *we* were...." he said slowly. "I'm not ready to lose you so quickly, not yet. Won't you at least think about it?Please."

"But I already have thought about it, Albert... I've thought about it a lot. It's really very simple. Very, very simple. Can't you see... it's the sacredness of life we're talking about... the sacredness of life."

He felt his heart contracting in his chest. He loved her so...

Another silence.

"But, of course, you are right, my dear... darling... Rachel... of course... It *is* the sacredness of life we're talking about..."

The sky was so very blue that day, so very blue.

Then, as if suddenly waking from a dream, he cried, "Rachel, come and stay with me at my house... please."

The sky was still so very blue.

She looked as if she was debating the idea in her mind but then she took a deep breath and said, "You were right all along, Albert. I have to go back to my son in Amsterdam."

When he heard those words, he turned on the engine and roared back to the hotel.

He didn't say another word, but there was real pain in his eyes when he kissed Rachel before she got out of the car and walked into the hotel.

"Damn!" Albert muttered to himself as he roared away from the hotel, leaving Rachel behind in the dust.

"Damn it to hell!"

He felt his hands clutching the steering wheel; he needed

something to hold on to that bad.

Never before had he wanted a woman the way he wanted Rachel. And now she was leaving him. Leaving him and Nice and going back to her husband and son in Amsterdam.

"Damn!"

There was too much traffic on the Promenade des Anglais on that October afternoon for him to speed away as fast as he'd wished, so he down-shifted his Porsche and tried to contain his energy. It wasn't easy for him to do; Albert Giovanni was a man who was used to getting what he wanted.But it wasn't happening this time and it was hard to believe. The woman he wanted, the woman he loved with all his heart, had turned and walked away.

But it's complicated. Of course it is. Way too complicated.

She's pregnant and doesn't even know who the father of the baby is...

Damn it to hell!

Maybe she would have stayed if she could have. But he knew she couldn't. She did have a son. It was the right thing to do... he knew it. He'd even said so from the beginning. She would have to go back because of her son.

But it didn't ease the pain.

But what about us? His mind was screaming. *What about what we'd just experienced together? What about...*

He was sure she loved him, quite sure – and he knew he loved her.

But she was pregnant. And she had a son.

Damn it to hell!

She left Nice in early October, and by late November, Albert still felt no better. He simply couldn't comprehend that she was gone. Gone!

It was as if his life had come to a standstill.

He couldn't concentrate, couldn't get his head around things, couldn't focus on work... he simply couldn't... couldn't, couldn't.... Days, weeks had gone by and it didn't stop – the aching inside, the turmoil in his mind.

Is it my karma? he kept asking himself. *My karma that I had to lose her because I so ruthlessly gave her to that brute Felix so he could fuck her front, back and sideways?* He cringed at the thought. *Is that what this is about? Is that what is really happening?* Yet he knew the logical explanation was that she was pregnant and went back to Amsterdam because of her son, but he was sure there was more to it than that. Quite sure.

And it tormented him every day of the week; he kept going over the story again and again. The story of how life had sent him this perfect angel, this perfect gem of a woman, and he'd thrown her to that beast. He just couldn't get it out of his head. *My behavior was unforgiveable* he kept thinking. *Unforgiveable!* Just the thought of Felix Fischer touching her, the thought of that lecher running his hands over her breasts, and penetrating her... the thought of that brute penetrating the woman he now knew he loved with all his heart and soul made him feel physically sick.

But the terrible images wouldn't go away. In his mind's eye he saw Felix assaulting her, touching and fucking her. It was making him crazy, mad...And to make matters worse, he felt his sex pulsing when he thought of Felix, running his hands down her abdomen and finding her warm pussy. Felix, with paws like a butcher, opening her tender bud and then bending down and kissing and licking her there with his ugly mouth. The thought made him desperate – made him feel like a pervert.

What was I thinking?

For the first time in his life, Albert realized that not only had he been ruthless and cruel, he had been careless with the precious gift life had given him. *Oh, God no,* he thought, trembling to think about the consequences of his actions. *The consequences! So this is what karma is all about. And to think I never understood it. Not before now.* He bowed his head in shame, ready to cry; but no tears came.

And now she was gone. Gone!

I'm really losing it… he thought. *Really…*

It was frightening. For the first time in his life, Albert Giovanni was actually floundering. *There must be something I can do,* his mind screamed. *Something. But what?* Day after day, he pondered this question – *What can I do? What?*

Finally, after weeks of torment, the answer came. All of a sudden, he knew what to do.

I have to get away, right now. Far, far away… if I don't want to lose it completely.

I have to do something else. I must… I simply must…

So he decided to drop everything and go to his master in Japan, immediately. He just had to. Just the thought of the mountains and meditating at his master's secluded retreat made him breathe easier. It would calm him, he was sure, and revive him. Even if he knew it would be hard because his mind was in such turmoil. But he also knew it would work, because he'd done it before. Meditated that is, the hard way. Until the mind finally calmed down. Then he would find solace, he was sure. Solace in the silence. And eventually maybe even hope. But no, he didn't want to go there. Not yet. He didn't want to get too far ahead of himself because he knew it would hurt.

No! What I need is silence and meditation and my master's calm, soothing presence.

He picked up the phone and called Victor Gandler, his right hand man, the man who was CEO of his worldwide operations at their head office in Vienna where all the practical aspects of his business empire were coordinated. After forty-five minutes on the phone with Victor, he'd given him a complete rundown of what he wanted done while he was away.

"I'll probably be gone for three or four weeks," he told Victor.

"OK," replied Victor Gandler tersely. He was used to his boss's high-flying lifestyle. It had been that way since they first met in 1985 when Albert, the prodigal son, finally returned from Japan. Victor was already working for Albert's father at that time.

Albert, for his part, had no worries about leaving things in Victor's hands; Victor had been running the company for years.

Next he called his travel agent to make the arrangements. First class to Japan – as soon as possible. There was just one more thing he needed to do – and that was talk to Stefan.

He stared at his computer screen; he realized he ought to send out a few more emails now that he was going away, but he couldn't. All he could do was imagine himself touching Rachel. He was obsessed with the thought of her. Obsessed with the woman he'd just lost. He could almost feel his hand sliding down her smooth abdomen to her warm, waiting pussy; that area of soft tenderness that he so desperately wanted now, and which he had so carelessly given to another man. He felt that shiver inside as he once again imagined Felix's fat fingers and disgusting mouth touching and tasting the soft lips of Rachel's pussy.

Ugh! How he hated himself for what he'd done, but still he couldn't help but wonder if she struggled against him?

Did she put up a fight against Felix's onslaught on her body, or did she just sigh and allow herself to open to Felix as she'd done with me?

It tormented him to wonder; it tormented him to think he'd never know… it tormented him…

Then he remembered how terrified she looked that night, right before he and Stefan left her alone with Felix at his condo. He had dragged her out into the hallway and pushed her up against the wall, feeling her breasts, her nipples taunt. The pure terror he saw in her innocent eyes haunted him to this day. She'd clung to him and begged him not to leave her with that disgusting man. Especially not after the incredible intimacy they'd shared; she obviously couldn't understand what was going on and why he was doing this to her. But he did it anyway.

It was almost as if it turned me on, giving her to that lecher like that. What a pervert I was! Did I really need that level of perversion and intensity to feel something…?

"Damn," he muttered to himself. "Damn it to hell!"

He turned off his computer (he wasn't looking at the screen anyway) and slammed down the lid. It would have to wait. Everything would have to wait.

For someone who'd been so proud of his ability to focus and control his mind, he damn well felt close to losing it now. Or maybe he already had. Lost it that is… lost control, lost his mind… lost her. Yes, there it was.

I've lost her. Lost her!

And there's nothing I can do about it. Nothing!

Except go to Japan and meditate.

But first dinner with Stefan.

He met Stefan at his usual table at Chez Paul, the same place where he'd first met Rachel that fateful night in late August, right after Stefan brought her to Nice.

How nonchalant and arrogant I was then, he thought as he sat down. *I thought Rachel would just be another one of Stefan's finds. Little did I know how different it would be this time!*

"So you're going to Japan? To meditate?" asked Stefan, looking up from his food after Albert told him he was leaving the next day.

When Albert nodded in assent, Stefan added quietly, "You love her, don't you?"

Stefan never talked much. That was his way. But he knew Albert, and knew him well. You could have heard a pin drop after he said those words.

Albert was silent for a moment; then he looked Stefan straight in the eye and said, "Yeah, I guess I do."

It was the first time they'd ever talked about Rachel like this. Up until then, Rachel was just another one of the many women he'd shared with Albert. But Stefan, despite his quiet ways, had been quick to pick up that something different was going on this time, something serious was happening between Rachel and Albert. He'd known it almost from the very beginning because he knew Albert, and he knew Rachel too. They were both people he loved, and loved deeply in his own quiet way. So even though he didn't say anything about it at the time – not to Albert or to Rachel – he'd seen what was going on between them, felt the intensity. And he remembered how Albert had sent him off to Cairo the night he'd given Rachel to that lecher Felix. He'd seen the pain in Albert's eyes as they drove away from his condo and knew something bad was happening, something despicable. Despicable for Albert and despicable for Rachel. But it wasn't his way to interfere. It never had been.

Then he saw how devastated Albert was after Rachel left Nice and went back to Amsterdam, even though Albert desperately tried to hide it from him. But he couldn't, his despair was too obvious. And for once, Albert wasn't interested in other women.

"Have your heard?" asked Stefan, breaking the silence, "My wife is coming to Nice with my daughters."

"Really?" exclaimed Albert in surprise. "For what? For a visit?"

"No, no, not for a visit. They're moving down here. Monique's willing to give our marriage another try. I've rented a house for us."

"That's wonderful," exclaimed Albert. He was truly happy for Stefan because he knew how much it pained him that he wasn't with his wife and daughters. So he added jokingly, "You're old enough to make a go of it this time, Stefan. Really!" Both men laughed.

The waiter came with their coffee and grappa.

After the waiter left, Albert said, "Tell me how you met Rachel. I'm curious."

"Oh, I met her quite by accident… on the beach – at Zandvoort – outside Amsterdam this past July. It was right after Monique threw me out for the umpteenth time. So I went to the beach, just to get away from it all. It was evening and the beach was almost deserted, but there she was, sitting there all alone, playing with her little boy."

Albert was silent for a while, as if lost in thought. Then he quietly finished briefing Stefan on the all things he wanted him to do while he was gone.

The last question Albert asked Stefan that evening was, "When exactly did Rachel get pregnant? Did she tell you?"

"She wasn't sure," replied Stefan, "but she said it was probably one of the very first days she was here in Nice."

Once Albert settled down into his first class seat on his Air France flight to Tokyo, he had time to contemplate what was waiting for him in Japan and he knew it would be hard, very hard. He saw himself sitting on his zafu, his meditation cushion, watching his breath, while his monkey mind ran wild. No... it wouldn't be fun, sitting on his cushion like that in his master's private zendo. But the real question was – would he be able to breathe and be present with no stories, no concepts? That was the real question. Funny when he thought about it, he knew instinctively that Rachel was closer to this state than he was, even with all his months and years of meditation practice. He just knew it and saw it in the way she regarded him with those green eyes of hers. She could just stand there and look and be present; she had that ability.

In his mind's eye, he saw the walls of his master's zendo, the zafus, and he could almost taste the pain. And the silence and the sitting and him facing the wall. He knew the drill only too well. He'd be watching his breath, watching and witnessing, while his thoughts ran wild. And Rachel would be with him, the whole time. He wouldn't be able to escape whatever was bothering him. He'd done it before so he knew what was in store...He saw himself, his thoughts running wild, facing the wall.

Yes, that was the way of it. Thirty-five minutes sitting

meditation or zazen, as they called it, ten minutes walking meditation, then another thirty-five minutes sitting meditation. Broken only by short breaks for simple food like rice and miso soup or some hard manual labor in the garden. Then back to his zafu and watching the breathing. Back to his thoughts running wild. Back to just observing it happen, without judging. Then for a moment, maybe a hair's breath of peace. Just maybe. For a moment, silence. Just maybe. Presence. Then his thoughts running wild again. The monkey mind, up and down, back and forth. He knew all its antics which was why he hated and loved his cushion already, even before he arrived. But he knew there was no other way for him if he wanted to calm down and get his life back.

Albert's sensei's most private and secluded monastery, where few people were ever admitted, was located some hundred and fifty kilometers outside Tokyo in the mountains. And that was where Albert was heading because his master, Okumara Sensei, was there at the moment. Albert wanted to be near his master. Not only did he want to feel his presence but he needed his guidance too.

The first two days after he arrived, Albert spent time with his master discussing the operation of his master's various Zen centers around the world, which Albert was helping support.

On the afternoon of the second day, his master said, "I go to New York in three months time. In February."

"Good," said Albert slowly; they were drinking tea together. Albert had been to the monastery in upstate New York many times over the years. He was also on the board of directors of the rehab center for drug addicts, which was connected to the monastery. The rehab center was run by Westerners who'd studied with Okumura Sensei in Japan and they were having good results with heroin addicts.

"One last time, I go," said his master. He was getting old. "To see my students… my most excellent students…"

"Good," said Albert again.

"You must come too," said Okumura Sensei. "You must be there too."

"Of course," replied Albert. He knew this was more than an ordinary request.

There was silence for a while.

Finally the old man said, "What brings you to Japan... this particular time? I sense something happened to you. Now you tell me."

Albert felt himself trembling slightly. This would be the first time he spoke the truth about what was in his heart out loud.

His master waited patiently, sipping his tea slowly.

Albert took a deep breath and then recounted his story and his feelings about Rachel, the woman he had lost.

The old man listened quietly, without interrupting. When Albert was done, his master didn't say a word. Instead he just sat there, unmovable like a mountain.

It was a great comfort to Albert that his beloved sensei had heard him, had listened to every word he said.

Then, after a long silence, his master said, "Now you go into retreat."

After ten days of silence, meditation and heavy work clearing, digging and planting trees and moving stones in the monastery's hidden gardens up and down the mountainside, Okumara Sensei called Albert in once again for an interview. This was a regular happening during retreats, so Albert didn't think much of it. Usually at such a session, the master might make some comments about one's meditation practice or give the student a koan to contemplate. But this time, when Albert entered the room, he sensed something unusual was about to happen. He bowed to his sensei and sat down in his usual place.

His master rang a little bell by his side and one of the young monks came in with tea. Albert waited in silence while his master poured the tea. He knew from experience that these things could not be rushed. He listened to fierce late November wind blowing outside as he sipped his tea slowly. It was almost December and there was snow in the air.

Suddenly his master set his cup down and cleared his throat. Albert put his cup down too and looked straight at Okumara Sensei and waited.

Then his master said, "Baby is yours. Go to her now and be father!" And with that he picked up his tiny tea cup and continued sipping his tea.

Albert looked at his master, thunderstruck.

What?

The baby is mine?

He felt the room fade in and out of his consciousness.

But, of course! Of course!

Why didn't I know?

Why hadn't I seen it?

Why hadn't I understood?

He had even asked Stefan the night before he left for Japan when Rachel got pregnant, and Stefan told him Rachel thought she probably got pregnant one of the first days she was in Nice. Why hadn't he understood it then? Why hadn't he remembered that he'd slept with her one of the very first days after she arrived in Nice? Why hadn't he remembered the power of that very first meeting and the passionate love they made that very first night?

That was the night! Of course!

Why didn't I remember?

Why didn't I understand that strange, powerful feeling I had after I drove her back to the hotel... Why didn't I realize something very special had happened...?

But now that his master had put all the pieces of the puzzle together for him, it made perfect sense.

The baby Rachel is carrying is mine!

Mine!

Of course!

He knew he was supposed to bow his head and continue sipping his tea, but he simply couldn't. He was that thunderstruck. He just couldn't move; rather it was as if the earth had moved. And then, when he finally realized that the earth had moved, he did bow his head.

The baby Rachel is carrying is mine. Mine!

So what am I doing sitting here, on some faraway mountaintop, somewhere in Japan, trying to meditate while the woman I love, the woman I adore, is struggling to make her way in the world, carrying my baby?

His master understood this too.

"Baby is yours. Now go," he said forcefully. "Go!"

Albert got up immediately, his legs shaking beneath him. He stood there for a moment; then he bowed, turned and left.

An hour later, he had packed his bags and left the monastery in his sensei's private car which sped him directly to Tokyo International Airport. Three days later, he was in Amsterdam.

As soon as Albert arrived in Amsterdam, he called Rachel.

"What are you doing in Amsterdam?" she cried, obviously surprised to hear from him, all of a sudden like that.

"Oh, just a little business," he said, his heart thumping in his chest. "And how are you, Rachel?"

"Well…" she hesitated, as if considering what to say. "Well… in fact, I'm packing up to go to New York with my mother and son."

"To New York? But what about your husband?"

"Well, we're not living together anymore… we're getting divorced."

"Oh, I see," he said slowly, feeling the warmth of this new information spread across his chest. "Rachel, let me take you to dinner tonight. Then you can tell me all about it, OK?"

When he picked her up at her apartment, he couldn't take his eyes off her. There she was. The woman he loved, with her wonderful, sumptuous chestnut hair. She was magnificent. *She's more magnificent than I remembered her* he thought. It took his breath away. But her mother, Isabel, was there and he had to make small talk with her instead of following his impulse to smother Rachel with kisses.

But the whole time he was chatting with Isabel, he felt her watching him with those incredible green eyes of hers. His heart swelled. *She still loves me!*

But something told him to proceed slowly and carefully.

So he took Rachel to dinner at the Grand Hotel where he was staying and talked softly with her about this and that, just enjoying her presence. After they'd eaten, he said, "Rachel, there's something important I want to talk to you about – and I can't do it here. Would you come up to my suite with me?"

She hesitated for a moment.

The energy between them was already intense. He knew she felt it. He wanted so much to hold her, touch her.

When they got to his suite, Rachel stood shyly over by the window looking out over Amsterdam while Albert hung her coat up. The he came up behind her and put his arms around her stomach as if it was the most natural thing in the world. She pulled away, turning towards him.

"Are you still pregnant?" he asked, smoothing down her luxurious chestnut hair.

"Yes. Yes, of course. What makes you think otherwise?"

"Well, it's difficult to see. You're still so thin… and well… women do change their minds…" he smiled and seemed thoughtful and hesitant.

"What did you want to talk to me about? Albert?"

He gazed out the window.

"Amsterdam is a beautiful city, it really is… but much too cold. How do you stand it?"

"Albert…"

"Rachel, I must know, could this baby be mine?"

She started to laugh but stopped abruptly as the thought penetrated and she realized what he was asking her. She looked stunned.

She walked over to the sofa and sat down abruptly as if she was trying to understand what he just said. Then she looked up at him with those incredible green eyes of hers. She didn't say a word.

He stood motionless, holding his breath.

"I never thought of it before… " she said slowly, "… never."

He pulled an armchair over and took her hands, waiting. He didn't say anything but gave her time. Time to digest the possibility.

Finally she replied, "Well, yes… yes, I guess so… the baby could be yours. But it could also be Stefan's."

"I thought so…" he said. "I thought it could be mine."

The room was so quiet you could have heard a pin drop.

"So walk me through the timeline, Rachel, will you," he said, suddenly very down to earth and businesslike, trying to hide the powerful emotions he was feeling. "When did you have your last period?"

She thought back. "August tenth."

"And when did you arrive in Nice?"

"August twentieth I think it was."

"Now let me see," he was checking his calendar. "Yes, here it is. We met for dinner that very first time at Chez Paul's on August twenty-fourth. Are your periods regular?" His tone was very matter-of-fact even though his heart was hammering in his chest.

"Yes," she replied. "Like clockwork."

"Well, then the night of the twenty-fourth, when we first made love, would have been the perfect time for you to get pregnant," he said slowly.

Rachel was silent again, trying to understand the ramifications of what he just said.

"Yes, I guess so." Her voice was almost a whisper.

"When is the baby due?"

"The doctor says May seventeenth based on me having my last period August tenth."

Albert took Rachel's hand again and said slowly, as if it was something he'd thought about saying for a long time, "Rachel, you know I'm not thirty, or even forty anymore. Life looks different to me now than it did before." She was watching him, listening quietly to what he was saying, obviously still in shock. "Can you understand that?"

All she did was nod.

"I didn't really think about it when Stefan first told me you were pregnant. But after you left and went back to Amsterdam, I couldn't forget it. I simply couldn't forget it – or you."

Rachel got up and started pacing the room, trying to get her bearings again after this incredible turn of events.

"But Albert, what if the baby is born with blond hair and blue eyes?"

"Well," he laughed, "then at least we'll know for sure that Stefan is the father."

She went over to the window and gazed out at the city, as if she was trying to grasp what was happening. He came up behind her and gently put his arms around her stomach. She nestled back into his chest and sighed softly.

Then he whispered in her ear, "The truth is, Rachel... I am sure, quite sure, this baby is mine."

She let him hold her for a while.

But then she left and went home to her mother.

He knew she would be back.

And now she was. Back.

Back at the Grand Hotel again with him. Only this time, she was in the big bed with him, her defenses finally down. He felt himself trembling with anticipation, standing on the brink, about to take the plunge into unknown territory. Only a few days before, he had been meditating on a distant mountaintop in faraway Japan, aching for her and now he was in Amsterdam, holding her in his arms. He almost couldn't believe his good fortune.

It was a miracle, a miracle indeed. And even more miraculous, she was holding him back, loving him back.

How did my sensei know? How?

He knew that people who are very high in consciousness often had extraordinary powers of clairvoyance, and now he was not in doubt that his old master did.

Did he also know that Rachel had already left her husband – and was just about to leave Amsterdam for good with her mother and son for New York? Perhaps he knew that too and it explained why his master had been so avid for him to leave immediately. Because the truth was he'd arrived in Amsterdam just in time to reach out and touch her again. Touch the woman he adored, and now she was there with him in the king-size bed at the Grand Hotel.

The evening before, when he'd asked her about the baby, she was so stunned that it made him feel strangely protective towards her. He wanted to be gentle and give her the time and space she needed to digest what was happening. So he was unruffled that her shock was so profound that she felt she had to go home to her mother to collect herself.

He knew it was okay and that she would be back.

And now she was, back in his arms again, all her defenses down, looking at him with those incredible green eyes of her. Present, real. The Rachel he loved. He might have been a man of the world his entire life, but at that very moment, he was no more. In fact, he'd never felt so unsure of himself, so vulnerable in his entire life… Never felt in over his head before, but now he did… and the intensity of his feelings for her left him awestruck.

The interesting thing was, Rachel read him like an open book and knew what he was feeling almost before he did… probably because she felt the same…the same awe, the same intensity, the same fear… as they lay together, trembling on the brink, him slowly and gently caressing her waiting body. And such was the power of the connection between them that the months of separation hadn't dimmed it at all; if anything, the separation had made it stronger.

Then, at that very moment when Albert hesitated, Rachel tossed her head and climbed up on top of him, laughing and kissing him passionately on the mouth.

He reveled in her kiss. There was a freedom and warmth in her that reminded him of home, of a home he'd always dreamed of but had never known.

But when their eyes met, he did know it. And he knew she understood what he was feeling, knew she was there, knew she was his woman, really and truly.

He wanted the moment to last forever.

Then he sighed and rolled over so he was on top of her again and he whispered in her ear, "Oh Rachel, you are safe with me, darling." A few moments later, when he could no longer contain himself, he plunged himself deep into her waiting pussy, finding her most secret places as she opened to him and received him, showering him with all the warmth and sweetness of her soul.

It was ecstasy beyond anything he'd ever experienced… as the world exploded and the miracle happened.

Later there were many kisses as they lingered in the big bed and he ran his hands over the softness of her exquisite body. *She is indeed magnificent. We are indeed magnificent* he thought and sighed. *And the baby she is carrying is mine!*

PART III

CAP FERRAT, THE FRENCH RIVIERA

It was almost mid-September, and more than a month had passed since Victor began blackmailing me into having sex with him. It was an awful situation and I was becoming more and more desperate and distraught as the days passed. But I simply couldn't figure out a way to escape the wicked trap he had set for me. Albert was still missing and Victor kept telling me that he and Prince Abdul were making real progress in their very delicate negotiations with Albert's abductors. But it all hinged on Victor paying the five million Euros in ransom for Albert's release, which he would only do if I had sex with him, whenever and however he wanted it. Oh how I detested the man! I simply despised him! Ugh! But I just didn't know how to escape…

Then one morning, he called to tell me of a change in his plans for his next sex fix with me.

"Rachel, I don't want you to come this afternoon, I want you to come this evening instead," he said. "Arrange for Amélie to sleep with the children tonight and come to the annex at nine."

"But why, Victor? What's going on?"

"You'll find out soon enough. Just come at nine, once the children are asleep," he said and hung up. I couldn't say I was thrilled, but I knew I had no choice.

For the first time, I seriously considered confiding in the housekeeper, Madam Raffin. I so desperately needed someone to talk to, but something made me hold back. There was just something about her – something a bit standoffish, something forbidding. If I needed an ally, she probably wasn't the right choice.

When I arrived at the annex that evening, Victor was waiting for me. He took my hand and led me through the offices to the guest house. As we entered the guest house, I realized I'd never actually been there before. For some reason, Albert had never shown it to me. I hadn't thought about it before, but now I wondered why Albert never took me there. But as soon as we entered, I knew why. There was just something about the place, something extravagant and decadent that felt all wrong. *What was Albert into before he met me?* I wondered. But I didn't have time to contemplate this question because to my great surprise, Madam Raffin was standing there in the opulent lounge, waiting for us.

Before I could say anything, Victor said, "Madam Raffin is going to prepare you for the evening. You can go with her."

"Hello, Rachel," Madam Raffin said softly, "come this way."

I was too surprised to say anything so I turned to follow her, wondering what this was all about. As we were leaving, Victor said, "I'll join you shortly, I'm just going to have a drink first."

I followed Madam Raffin down the hall.

She opened the door to a large, lavish-looking bathroom/ dressing room. In the middle of the room, there was a black marble Jacuzzi. On one side of the Jacuzzi, there was a posh red sofa and two swanky red armchairs. On the other side of the Jacuzzi was an elegant and well-stocked dressing table and next to that, a clothes rack with lingerie and other items hanging from it.

"Get undressed, Rachel," said Madam Raffin. "We are going to start by bathing you first."

"We?"

"Just get undressed, Rachel."

There was nothing chatty about Madam Raffin, nothing at all. If I had any illusions about being able to talk to her, they completely evaporated in the warm air of the dressing room.

While I was undressing, Victor came in and sat down on one of the red armchairs to watch. Madam Raffin had already filled the Jacuzzi, so now she just checked the water to make sure the temperature was exactly right.

When I was naked she pinned my hair up on top of my head

and said, "Get in."

I slid slowly into the warm water.

Aaahhh… if nothing else… the bath was lovely and warm.

After I had been in for a few minutes, Madam Raffin said, "Now stand up."

When I was standing, she rolled up the sleeves of her dress and sponged me all over, slowly and carefully, as Victor watched. He was obviously satisfied with what he saw and twirled the ice cubes in his glass more and more excitedly as Madam Raffin gently washed my most private parts. What surprised me most was how slowly and carefully she touched me. It was all rather sensual and unexpected from her; the woman I had been calling the Ice Queen. It was almost as if she was enjoying herself.

"She's beautiful, isn't she?" said Victor.

"Mais oui!" said Madam Raffin softly, touching my warm pussy with her fingertips.

When she was done, Madam Raffin told me to get out of the bath and then she towel dried me vigorously. When I was dry, she carefully massaged my breasts and buttocks with delicious rose-scented oil.

"I want to see her in the black corset," Victor said, now obviously excited and getting impatient.

"Not so fast," she replied, "I want to make her up first and she must have the red nail polish. Otherwise you will not enjoy her in the black corset so much, you know that!"

The way she spoke told me they had done this before.

It made me wonder if Albert had participated in things like this…

But she didn't give me time to think; instead she led me over to the dressing table and told me to sit down. Victor came over and stood behind me. He started touching my breasts, fondling my nipples the way he knew I liked.

"Victor, go and get some fresh air," Madam Raffin said firmly.

"And come back in twenty minutes."

To my great surprise, he didn't protest, but did as she said.

When he was gone, she stood behind me and ran her fingers slowly up and down my neck, very gently. Then she put her hands on my breasts and held them for a moment as she contemplated me in the mirror. "You will look lovely in the corset I have chosen for you. But first we must do your nails. The nails are important, you know." With that, she pulled up a stool and sat down beside me and polished my fingernails and toenails a deep, dark red. Then she quickly powdered my face and finally, she took the red lipstick and colored first my lips and then my nipples. When she was satisfied, she went and got the black corset from the clothes rack and told me to stand up.

The corset was old-fashioned and made of beautiful, black lace. It was the kind of corset that laced up in the back, so Madam Raffin turned me around and laced me up from behind, pulling my waist in tightly. The corset lifted up my breasts, but didn't cover them. Rather they were even more exposed, which seemed to please Madam Raffin no end. I had no panties on either, just the corset. When I was laced up, Madam Raffin turned me around, surveying how I looked with satisfaction.

Then, to my great surprise, she took my breasts in her hands and bent forward and started kissing them. Her kisses were so soft and tender, almost passionate. I was amazed. So gentle and sensual was her touch that I heard myself moan with pleasure.

I couldn't believe that this was Madam Raffin, the Ice Queen herself, the woman I had thought was so unsympathetic, the woman I had felt was so distant and unfriendly.

At that very moment, the door opened and Victor walked in. He didn't like what he saw.

"Now, now, Claudia," he said. "We'll have none of that, please. You know she's mine."

Madam Raffin released my breasts immediately and stepped back without a word.

"That will be all for now," he said, dismissing her with a wave of his hand.

Madam Raffin straightened my hair gently and I trembled at her touch. Then she turned and left, closing the door quietly behind her.

Victor was upon me immediately, ready to devour me. He began touching my uplifted breasts, saying, "Your breasts are so incredible. Incredible!" Then he was kissing them, but his touch was nothing compared to Madam Raffin's gentleness. She had aroused me in just a moment in a way he never could.

"Come," he cried, taking my arm and leading me out of the dressing room into the adjoining bedroom. Now he was in a hurry, unbuttoning his shirt and holding me to his bare chest so that my bare breasts rubbed up against him. He liked that.

He began kissing my neck as he undid my hair which fell down around my face, touching my upturned breasts. He pulled away and regarded my taunt red-painted nipples and then leaned forward and took first the one in his mouth and then the other, sucking them hard and biting them until I began to moan. He knew from experience that I liked it like that.

Then he backed away and took my taunt nipples and squeezed them hard with his fingers until I moaned some more.

My pussy was wet; I no longer resisted Victor as I had done in the beginning. In fact, I had become his slave – and he knew it. Knew he could do with me whatever he wanted and I wouldn't resist.

When he was satisfied that I was wet enough and excited enough, he pushed me back onto the big satin bed and took off his trousers as he regarded me lying there, completely naked except for the tight black corset. It obviously excited him to see me like that and he stood there naked, looking at me with his erect penis pulsing in the air. He had a severe air about him; it was almost as if he was an inquisitional priest with his insane, fiery eyes. He was truly a man possessed and I could see he liked seeing me in the corset so much that he was going to fuck me with it on.

He came towards me and I knew it would turn him on even more to be able to hold me tightly at my corseted waist. But what I hadn't expected was that he would want to bind my wrists to the headstand of the bed first. But that's exactly what he did.

"Give me your hand," he said, reaching for my left arm. He pulled out a soft, red, silk wrist cuff from the side table and tied my left wrist expertly to the headstand. Then he went around to the other side, and tied my right wrist with the other red wrist cuff to the headstand.

"Now, Rachel, you belong to me," he said as he spread my legs apart and began touching my pussy. "Tonight I am going to make you beg for mercy! Tonight... but first..."

He was so excited by me and the corset and having me bound like that, that he could no longer contain himself. So he mounted me and cried, growling deeply, "Oh, Rachel... now you are mine, mine!" I felt him deep inside me, bearing down on me, plunging headlong into a place he'd never been before.

It was as if, being bound and corseted as I was, I had awakened an unexpected fierceness in him, a passion he'd never experienced before. So he buried himself deep in my waiting pussy, which was already aroused by Madam Raffin's gentle caresses. And because of Madam Raffin, my pussy was warm and wet in a way she usually wasn't for him, which turned him on even more. And since I was bound, he did not have to worry about my arms but could hold me tightly around my waist, squeezing me to him.

"Oh, Rachel," he growled hoarsely as he moved his cock around in me, grunting with pleasure.

The red nails, the black lace corset, the rose-scented oil had all done their work. Everything about me was driving him mad with desire and there he was, finally, twisting and thrusting himself deep inside me. I felt myself once again, letting go and surrendering to the inevitable. Surrendering to my fate, until I heard myself moaning with him. Then my hips began to sway as good pussy bad pussy followed his pounding rhythm until he exploded inside me, bellowing like a fierce animal in the night...

But that was only the beginning. Later that night he did more to me, so much more; licking and caressing my aching pussy while I was bound to the bed. Yes, he bound my legs to the bedposts too. Once I was spread-eagle like that, he put his hungry lips to my sensitive inner labia, tasting them and sucking them until I was moaning with pleasure. And he kept on sucking, sucking intensely, making me feel open and exposed, bare and completely defenseless before him until I surrendered myself to him, climaxing powerfully in his mouth.

But even after that, he refused to let me rest. Instead, he took his fingers and began massaging my clitoris and my little pussy's aroused inner lips softly and gently. Softly and gently, oh ever so softly and gently, and he wouldn't stop. Back and forth and back and forth, he massaged and rubbed me. Softly and gently, then softly and quickly, until I simply had to let go and surrender one more time. Moreover, being bound as I was, there was absolutely nothing I could do to resist the powerful waves of sensation his touch aroused in me. I didn't know my tormentor could be so gentle. Oh no, and my little pussy, she was aching and reeling and had me begging for mercy. But there was none. No mercy, no rest. He had me exactly where he wanted me and was in full control. He was the master, the insane, inquisitional tormentor who enjoyed pushing me until at last I was crying out with pleasure again, even though I hated and despised him.

So once more, this madman had cornered me and forced me into submission, driving me to do his bidding.

And even when the tears were flowing, he refused to let me go. Instead, he pushed me even further by gently and tenderly caressing my quivering, exhausted body with a feather. He ran the feather ever so lightly and softly up and down my thighs and across my belly, again and again. And still he wouldn't stop. But this time, the softness of the feather surprised me and made me relax a little and so he continued. Continued to push me and awaken sensations in me that I did not know he could find.

And when I was open and moaning again, he put his fingers in me once more and then with his lips to my pussy and his fingers in my ass, he pushed me and pushed me, calling me "bitch", "whore", "slut", and other horrible names, humiliating me until I no longer knew who I was...

So Victor had his way with me all through the night, teasing me and egging me on and then caressing me gently. Finally, when I thought I could take no more, he put his face right up to mine, and holding my head in his hands, he said, "Rachel, tell me you want me to fuck you. Tell me. I want to hear you say it."

When I spoke no word, he said, "Say it, Rachel; I won't let you go until you do. I promise you, I won't. I want to hear you say it. Come now!

He pinched my nipples hard and I felt the hatred flare up in me again. I wanted to spit in his face; but didn't dare.

"Come now, say it!" he cried. There was a strange urgency in his voice. "I'm not going to untie you until you do."

I hated him so much that I wept, but still he held me.

"Say it," he hissed at me.

"Victor," I heard myself whisper, "fuck me..."

"Louder," he cried. "Say it louder!"

"Fuck me."

"Louder!"

"Fuck me!"

"And say please!"

"Please... "

"Please fuck me!"

"Louder!"

"Victor, please fuck me!"

Finally, when I had begged and pleaded enough to satisfy him, he entered me one last time and fucked me until he was absolutely sure he had conquered me completely.

Then he untied me and I wept.

And he held me and caressed me with a gentleness I didn't know he possessed.

Which only made me weep more.

And whether I wept from the sheer exhaustion of it all or from this sudden kindness from my tormentor, I did not know.

All I knew was that for a little while, there was strange feeling of peace and tranquility between us, and an uncanny stillness which my battered soul so longed for.

For a while, I dozed in his arms, my troubles forgotten.

But then he woke me and broke the spell when he said, as he began caressing my breasts again, "If Albert doesn't come back to you alive, Rachel, I promise you, I'll look after you."

And I hated him more than ever before.

When finally he fell asleep, I got up from the bed and looked at him and hated him with all my heart. I wanted to spit on him but didn't dare. *What if he wakes up?* No it wasn't worth the risk. So instead, I hissed "I hate you! I hate you! I hate you, you filthy bastard!" and left.

I staggered back up to the house and threw myself onto our big empty bed and cried my heart out, feeling lost and miserable. I just couldn't understand what was going on. Couldn't understand why this was happening.

What is it with me? I thought. *What is it with me and men and the sexual experience?*

How could I have orgasm with a man I detested so much? When I thought about what Victor had done to me – how he blackmailed me and abused me and forced me to do what he wanted – how could I have orgasm with a man like that? How? And not only that, how could I actually enjoy it when it happened? It made me cringe to think about it. But there was just something about having an orgasm... something about the physical sensations and the orgasmic experience itself that was way beyond my logical mind. And way beyond my hatred for him as well. It was as if my body and my pussy just took over and the pleasurable sensations were undeniable and unstoppable even if I despised the man. So despite what my mind was screaming, my body could come over and over again with someone I hated so much.

I winced at the thought of it. At the thought of me! At the thought of what was happening to me. What was I doing? What was wrong with me? Was I sick? Demented? Insane? What was it with me? Or was it just that I was so tormented by the whole situation and so desperate because of Albert's abduction that I'd lost all sense of right and wrong? The whole situation was so grotesque and degrading; I knew what I was doing was so degrading. It just was. It was shameful and humiliating... *If only I'd protested a little more* I thought. Then it wouldn't have been so shameful.

But how could I? How could I protest? Victor had made it abundantly clear that if I didn't cooperate and cooperate completely, he'd refuse to pay the ransom money. It was as simple as that. I had no choice really, none whatsoever. Victor had even told me two days before that he had spoken to Prince Abdul again and the Prince had told him they were actually negotiating with the kidnappers to arrange for delivery of the five million Euros!

So, in fact, I should be celebrating. Celebrating because that meant Albert was alive and maybe he'd even be home soon. Back home. Alive and free again!

But how could that be? Would Victor really let that happen now that he had me? The man was so obsessed with me. Obsessed.

I sat up in the bed, in a cold sweat.

Suddenly nothing made sense.

What will Victor do if Albert really does come back? I thought.

I felt sick to my stomach.

Then it hit me: *What will Albert do when he finds out what Victor did to me while he was gone?*

Oh, God no... could it be?

I simply didn't know what to think... I simply didn't know what to make of it. *What – oh, what is going on?* I didn't know. *Oh, God no... could it be?*

So I lay there... all bunched up in a big ball, holding my stomach, in the big bed in Albert's big house, suddenly cold as ice. *What is Victor up to? What is he up to? Oh, God no...*

I cringed and cried and hated myself even more and felt even more guilty and disgusted with myself for being so lascivious that night in that tight black corset with my red nipples and red nails and for coming so many times with that despicable man.

And that was how Madam Raffin found me – all bunched up in a ball in the middle of the bed, holding my stomach and crying my heart out.

I didn't know she was there until I felt her gentle touch on my head and heard her soothing voice saying, "Now, now, now, Rachel, everything's going to be okay. Everything's going to be okay, I promise you." And with that, she slipped into the bed beside me and undid the corset. Then she pulled me into her arms and held me as I cried myself to sleep.

It was the sound of Madam Raffin pulling back the curtains that woke me up the next morning. My first thought was *I have to find out the truth. I have to figure out what Victor's really up to.*

When I opened my eyes, I discovered Madam Raffin was standing there with a breakfast tray for me – with lovely toast, a soft boiled egg, and a pot with steaming hot tea.

I smiled thankfully in her direction, not quite knowing what to make of her or the situation. I looked at the clock by the bedside, *Oh my God, it's nine thirty – the children must be up.*

"Don't worry," said Madam Raffin, reading my mind, "Amélie is looking after the children. She'll take Isabella with her when she takes Daniel to playschool. Now eat some breakfast."

I pushed my hair back and did as she said. I was famished.

She didn't say anything as I ate, but she didn't leave either. She just stood there, watching me.

When I finished the egg and toast and began sipping the tea, I said, "Thank you."

She smiled softly and when she did, it all came flooding back to me. How she had crept into my bed the night before and comforted me. "And thank you for last night," I said slowly and then I added, patting the bed next to me. "Won't you sit down and talk to me?"

She looked startled.

"Please, Claudia." It was the first time I'd called her by her first name.

She looked even more startled and came over and sat down next to me on the bed.

"How much do you know about Victor?" I asked, plunging right in.

"What do you mean?" she replied. I could see I caught her off guard.

"I mean how well do you know him?"

She hesitated for a moment and then she said, "Well, I know that Albert never really liked him or trusted him."

When she said those words, I started to cry.

Now it was me who was caught off guard.

"Really?" I said through my tears. "I thought he was Albert's right hand man."

"Oh, he is, but it's not like you think. You see, it's because he worked for Albert's father during those years – those four, long years – when Albert was in that Zen monastery in Japan."

That was a bit of news. I stopped crying and looked at her in surprise. When I didn't say anything, she continued. "During those four, long years, Victor became like Bernardo's second son – the son he always wanted Albert to be – a dutiful, hardworking businessman. It wasn't easy for Albert when he came back from Japan."

"How do you know so much?"

"Oh, I've been with the family for many years. You see, I was already working here at the house while Albert was in Japan. I remember I just turned twenty-five when Albert returned in 1985. He was only twenty-three then. It was the year his sister died..." her voice trailed off.

"Carlotta?" I said.

"Yes," she replied slowly. "It was such a tragedy."

"Albert never really told me much about it... so much was happening in our lives... we had so little time together..." I started crying again. "What happened to her? I thought she died in a car crash."

"Yes, she did, poor girl. She was only twenty at the time. She was the apple of her father's eye. He simply doted on her and spoiled her – especially with Albert being gone. She was such a beautiful girl, but she was wild, a party girl and their father – Bernardo – well, he simply didn't want to see it or know about it. The drugs, the boyfriends, the partying, the alcohol. He simply refused to believe that his beloved daughter was like that. It was just more than he could bear or cope with; he loved her so much and he was so old-fashioned.

"I still remember that terrible night when it happened. I wasn't the head housekeeper then, but I was a member of the staff. It was summertime and the whole family was here at the house. And Carlotta, she was always out, partying with her friends, living the life – often until late at night. Sometimes her father would scold her, but she always just laughed at him. She had a way with him, a way of rolling her eyes and laughing and kissing him on the cheek and saying 'Oh, Papa!' that he couldn't resist."

She paused for a moment and then plunged on. "Then there was that terrible night when she didn't come home. It was very late and Bernardo was pacing the floor as he often did when she came home late. Because even if she didn't know or care, her father never went to bed until he knew she was home safe. But on that terrible night, she didn't come home at all, but the police did. I still remember that awful howl! How Bernardo howled when he heard the news. It was terrible, terrible! He sounded like a wounded animal… And then he simply stalked out of the house and walked into the night. No one tried to follow him. Not even Albert's mother, Beatrice; she just sat there on the sofa, sobbing. No one saw Bernardo come back either. But the staff whispered that he came back, many, many hours later. All I knew was that he was a changed man from that day on. He never spoke Carlotta's name again."

I was surprised to see tears in Madam Raffin's eyes.

"So you see, Rachel, it wasn't easy for Albert when he returned from Japan. Carlotta was dead, his father was a changed, bitter man, and Victor was pretty much running the show."

We sat in silence for a while as she dried her eyes and I tried to digest what she'd just told me.

Then I blurted out, "You know Victor has been blackmailing me to sleep with him!"

"What?" she exclaimed in surprise. "How can he do that?"

"Oh, it's easy," I cried, "He told me he wouldn't pay the five million Euros in ransom for Albert's release unless I do exactly what he says. Did you really think I was sleeping with him because I wanted to?"

"Oh, my God," she cried, jumping up from the bed in shock. "That bastard!"

"So you thought I was sleeping with him because I wanted to? Claudia! How could you believe that of me? I love Albert. You must know that. You must have seen how devastated I've been…

and am..."

"Yes, it's true," she replied slowly, sitting back down on the bed. "It didn't really make much sense to me; but then again, I kept saying to myself that I didn't really know you. And then when I saw you were sleeping with Stefan... well, to be honest, I just didn't know what to think."

"Oh, I see," I replied thoughtfully. "Then you probably don't know that I was with Stefan before I met Albert. Stefan and I were in love and we were having a relationship. We met in Amsterdam; he was separated from his wife at the time and I'd left my husband and we were together. In fact, it was Stefan who first brought me to Nice and who introduced me to Albert."

"Oh, I see," she said. "I didn't know."

"No, how could you? But the truth is I love Stefan too... and I always will. And both Stefan and I love Albert. It might be hard for you to understand, but that's just how it is. Stefan and Albert... " I said slowly and then I began to cry again.

She moved closer and took my hand and stroked it gently.

I looked up at her through my tears. "We've got to find out what Victor is really up to. He told me two days ago that Prince Abdul said his people were making progress in the delicate negotiations they were having with Albert's kidnappers, and that they were now close to arranging a delivery drop for the five million Euros."

"But what about the Foreign Ministry?" asked Claudia.

"That's exactly what I said. But Victor said – from the very first time he mentioned all this to me – that this was something Prince Abdul was working on privately. And that under no circumstances was I to mention any of this to the Foreign Ministry or to anyone else. Now I'm suddenly beginning to wonder if there's any truth to any of this. Because if it is true and Albert does come back – well where does that leave Victor? Especially when Albert finds out what Victor has done to me... how he..."

"Yes, I see," said Claudia slowly, "I see…"

"Because the last time I spoke to Jacques Durand from the Foreign Ministry, he said they'd completely lost contact with Albert's kidnappers and that I should prepare myself for the worst. You remember that, don't you? It was the end of June and now it's September."

"Yes, of course I do," she said.

"Since then I've heard nothing more from the Foreign Ministry – nothing. And now for the last few weeks, Victor has been offering me the hope that Albert is alive and that they are talking again to his kidnappers about the ransom money. And then there is the small matter of him wanting to fuck me. Damn it to hell!" I cried.

Now that she finally understood what was really going on, Claudia was absolutely livid and wanted to help me.

"This is just so awful, Rachel," she cried angrily. "We have to find out what's going on."

Hearing her words, I felt a sudden surge of energy course through my body and I jumped out of bed. Now finally, I had an ally.

The clock by the bed said quarter past ten.

"Victor left early this morning for Vienna and Munich, you know," she said thoughtfully.

"Yes, I know. He said he'd be gone until the middle of the week. So that gives us some time," I cried pulling on my jeans and a t-shirt and rushing out to the bathroom to pee and brush my teeth. "Let's go check his office."

"Don't you want to shower first?" asked Claudia.

"No," I cried, "this is more important. There's no time to lose."

I was already out in the hallway, running down the stairs. Claudia was right behind me – as furious and energized as I was.

"That bastard," I kept muttering under my breath. "Bastard!"

Once inside the annex, it didn't take long to realize that Victor had taken his laptop with him. So if there were any emails we should see, there was no way we could. Besides, we both realized rather quickly, he wouldn't communicate with the Prince by email anyway. It would be by phone, and of course he had his phone with him.

There were very few papers on his desk, and those that lay there were just innocent notes or orders from various contacts. Nothing of interest. When we looked through his drawers, it was the same. In this day of the electronic office and online business, there were very few papers anywhere, and least of all here where Victor sat wheeling and dealing all day long by phone.

"Maybe there's something on his backup computer," said Claudia.

"Does he have one?" I asked.

"Yes, he keeps it in one of the back rooms. Come, I'll show you."

She led me to a smaller office further down the hall.

"In the old days, Victor sometimes worked here. That's why his old computer is still here. Only today he uses it to backup documents he wants to keep. At least that's what he told me."

She turned on the computer.

"Damn!" she cried once it was fired up. "It's password protected, of course. I should have known."

We looked at each other, feeling deflated. Our initial feeling of optimism had disappeared. We headed back to the main office.

"There must be a way we can get in touch with Prince Abdul," I cried. "He's the only one who can tell us if there's any truth to what Victor's been saying."

"Yes, you're right. But how can we get his number," said Claudia. "Saudi princes are not that easy to get in touch with. In fact, they are always surrounded by a wall of security and bodyguards."

We were both silent for a moment, pondering the question.

"There must be a way," I said.

"What about calling Jacques Durand at the Foreign Ministry?" asked Claudia.

"But Victor made me swear not to tell him."

"Yes I know, but what if Victor's lying... and more importantly, Jacques will know how to get in touch with the Prince."

I was silent for a moment, thinking about what she said.

"If only we could get in touch with Prince Abdul without calling Jacques..." I said, feeling uneasy and unsure about to what to do next. I looked at the room with its beautiful décor and couches but I didn't want to sit down on any of them. I didn't want to be in contact with any of the couches where Victor had touched me and felt me and fucked me so often.

"Ugh! Let's get out of here," I cried, pushing the doors open to the lawn.

From the look on her face, I knew Claudia knew what I was feeling.

Now she was beginning to understand the degree of the degradation I had suffered.

"Merde!" was all she could say as we stepped out into the bright sunshine.

Once outside, I found myself gulping for air. For a moment I thought I was going to vomit. But the sickly sensation passed.

"Come," said Claudia, taking my hand firmly. "A nice cup of tea will do you good."

We sat and drank tea in the kitchen without speaking; both wondering what to do next.

Finally Claudia broke the silence. "You're sure you don't want to call Jacques Durand?"

I put my head in my hands and sighed. I felt completely drained all of a sudden and just didn't know what to think. "We're talking about Albert's life, Claudia," I cried. "I can't afford to make a mistake."

"You're right," she replied softly, and then added, "I can see you're too exhausted to think straight, Rachel. Why don't you go up and get some sleep before Daniel comes home from playschool. We don't have to decide anything right this minute. And besides, I have something I want to look into anyway which might help us. So why don't you go up and rest a little?"

When I didn't move, she added. "Victor won't be back for a few more days, so we have some time. Now go up and take a nap, Rachel. It's not going to help if you collapse."

She was right; I was totally and utterly exhausted.

I got up and went to our bedroom and fell immediately into a dark, dreamless sleep.

When I got up, Claudia told me about the recordings she'd been making of Victor's conversations. At first I was shocked, but when she explained what she'd been up to, I liked her even more.

"After Albert was kidnapped, I started feeling more and more insecure about my own position here at the house since I've never liked Victor and previously had trouble with him. So as a kind of insurance, I hired some technicians to set up a recording system in the main office. I told them Albert wanted this installed to record meetings. Once the system was set up with the tiny microphones hidden from view, I started recording every day because I was hoping to find something I could use in case Victor tried to force me out of the house. So while you were sleeping I listened to the recordings in the hope I would find something we could use – and you know what I discovered, Rachel? I discovered I had recorded the conversation you had with Victor when he blackmailed you into sleeping with him. What a despicable man, Rachel! I simply can't believe it. Ugh! I'd like to rip the balls off the bastard! But the good news, Rachel, is – this means we have proof. Proof that he blackmailed you. Proof! And that means we can go to the police…"

"Proof…" I whispered softly after her. "Proof. But how will this affect the situation with Albert?"

"Well, if Victor is arrested, someone else will have to be temporarily appointed to be operational director of Giovanni International, and whoever that is will then have access to the money we need to pay Albert's ransom."

"Oh, Claudia," I cried, tears suddenly running down my cheeks, "you're such an angel!" I threw my arms around her. "Let's go to the police right away."

She looked at her watch. "It's Saturday afternoon... so it's too late to go now," she said. "All the detectives will be gone for the weekend. There will only be a few rookies on duty now and we need to talk to someone with some authority. This is a very serious matter; it's Victor Gandler we're talking about..."

"Oh," I said softly, feeling strangely deflated.

"We'll go first thing Monday morning – before Victor gets back."

But then the expected happened. At four o'clock Sunday afternoon, Victor returned to the house with Felix Fischer. I saw the car pull up from my bedroom window.

"Oh God, no!" I cried out loud to no one in particular. I picked up the house phone and Claudia answered immediately. She too had seen the car. "What are we going to do?" I cried.

"I promise you, I won't abandon you, Rachel. No matter what happens. Victor's buzzed me so I've got to run." The line went dead.

I was in a panic.

Victor was back – with Felix! I felt my heart pounding in my chest.

Felix Fischer! Another lecher!

I didn't know which of the two men I despised most – Victor or Felix.

I felt hot and cold all over.

What if...

What if they both want to fuck me?

A half hour later, Claudia was in my room telling me that Victor wanted her to prepare me like she did the last time for another evening of dalliance…

"Claudia, I can't do it! I just can't," I cried. "And now he's got Felix with him. What if he wants to fuck me too?"

"I know, I know," she said softly and took my hand, patting it ineffectively.

I jumped up and ran over to my closet and started grabbing some clothes. "I'm going to leave right now," I cried. "I've just got to get away."

"But Rachel, what about your children?" Claudia exclaimed.

"I'll take them with me. Of course!" I cried.

But then I stopped cold in my tracks; Amélie had taken Daniel and Isabella out for the afternoon to a children's carnival with her sister and her sister's children.

"I've got to go anyway," I cried. "Amélie can look after them…"

"You can't go without your children, Rachel," cried Claudia heatedly. "You just can't!"

"Oh God, he wouldn't do anything to my children, would he?"

"I am afraid he would, Rachel, I'm afraid you have no idea how vicious Victor Gandler can be if he doesn't get what he wants… Trust me; I know what I'm talking about." The way she said it made my blood turn cold.

"Oh God, no!" I cried in a panic. "What are we going to do?"

Claudia was silent for a moment as if she was thinking. Then she pointed to the bed and said, "Come and sit down, Rachel, I think I have an idea.

"It's important we don't do anything to arouse Victor's suspicions. If he gets suspicious, there's no telling what he'll do. So let's go through with the preparations just like we did last time I prepared you," she said. "Only this time, I'll get word to Amélie to take your children to her mother's house outside Nice to spend the night there. So we're sure they're out of harm's way. And then, once I've prepared you, I'll slip out and call the police.

"If we do it this way," she continued convincingly, "the police will arrive just when Victor and Felix have tied you to the bed… so they'll barge in just when the two of them are beginning to work you over. And this – combined with the evidence I have of the recorded conversation – well, that should be more than enough to get Victor locked up."

Before I could protest, Victor buzzed her again and she had to rush off.

She left me there, shivering all over.

I hope to God she's right, I thought, *but what if something goes wrong?*

So there I was, back in the Jacuzzi in the House of Sin and Claudia was bathing me again as she had done before, with the same infinite gentleness. And despite my fear of what soon might happen, I could not help but enjoy her touch. It was so soft and tender; kinder than any man's. I knew that she truly cared for me and would do whatever she could to protect me. Which comforted me greatly, trapped as I was, in the House of Sin again.

After she got me out of the bath and dried me slowly and carefully, she meticulously massaged me again with that wonderful, delicious rose-scented oil, paying special attention to my breasts which seemed to delight her no end. Fortunately for us, Victor was not there this time and I allowed myself to enjoy the pleasure of her gentle touch.

I sighed and so did she.

"Claudia," I whispered softly, "promise me you won't let them go on too long…"

"Oh, my dear Rachel," she cried, "I…." but she didn't get to finish because Victor came barging across the room shouting, "You what?" Claudia and I had been so lost in our own world that we failed to notice that Victor and Felix had slipped quietly into the room.

Victor slapped Claudia viciously across the face.

"What kind of silly notions are you putting into Rachel's head?" he roared. Claudia flinched and turned deathly pale, but she didn't say a word.

"Now get her in that corset before I really lose my temper!" he continued.

I'd never seen him like that before; I shivered all over.

Claudia turned and went over to the clothes rack for the black corset.

"And I want her nipples and mouth painted red like last time," he barked. "Felix and I will be back in ten minutes and she'd better be ready!"

They left, slamming the door.

I started to cry.

"Shhh...." Claudia said as she hurriedly painted my nipples and mouth. A welt was already forming on her cheek where he'd hit her. "Come, let's get you into this corset."

She began lacing me up from behind.

I had the feeling she was crying softly, but I didn't dare move.

I wondered what kind of a hold Victor had over Claudia. It must have been really something; otherwise she'd never let him treat her like this...

Before I had time to speculate more, Victor and Felix returned with drinks in their hands; they both seemed in a jolly mood. Victor came over to me and inspected me. He loosened my hair so it fell down to my breasts. I could tell by the lust in his eyes that he was pleased with what he saw. Then he took me by the hand and led me over to Felix.

"Now isn't she just gorgeous?" he said proudly to Felix as if I was a priced possession. "Rachel, you remember Felix, I am sure. Why don't you entertain him for a moment while I have a word with Madam Raffin."

Then he nudged me toward Felix who grabbed me by my

tightly corseted waist and pulled me to him. He was as big and bear-like as I remembered him to be. I felt one of his big paws clutch my bare bottom.

"Aaahh, Rachel!" he said, keeping his hand on my bare buttock and almost growling. "More beautiful, more beautiful!" was all he could say. I remembered he couldn't speak English.

He sat down on one of the red chairs and pulled me down on his knee. He chuckled to himself as he began fondling my breasts, pinching and pulling my nipples.

"Ouch!" I cried; he was just as rough and uncouth as he was the last time I was with him.

He laughed – ever the lecher.

Victor, who had left the room with Claudia, came back alone and walked over to us, twirling a key chain with one little key on it. He dangled the key before me and said, "Well, I've locked Madam Raffin in the storage room – just to be on the safe side. We wouldn't want her to disturb our fun now, would we?"

I felt myself turn pale. *Locked in the storage room! Oh no! That means she won't be able to call the police… that means…*

When Victor saw me turn pale like that he said, "Now, now, there's nothing to worry about, Rachel. I'm sure she'll be perfectly fine in there for the next couple of hours. If you're a good girl, I promise you, I'll give you the key when we're done. Now come, let's go to the bedroom. I want to tie you up so Felix and I can really enjoy you."

Oh God, what am I going to do?

"I want to go back to the house!" I cried, panicking suddenly. "I don't want to…"

"Go?" said Victor, grabbing my arm firmly. "Whatever do you mean, Rachel…"

"I don't want to! Let me go…" I cried hysterically, almost screaming, "I've had enough… please…Let me go…" I struggled to free myself from Victor's grip but he held on to me tightly. I tried to pull away but Felix grabbed my other arm and they started dragging me towards the bedroom.

"Let me go," I cried and struggled with all my might, but with Felix holding me on one side and Victor on the other, there was nothing I could do to escape these two men.

"Please don't do this..." I cried, "I don't want to... how can you? Let me go!" But I knew it wouldn't help. Even if I screamed louder, no one would hear me down there at the annex – no one was up at the house anyway... Victor and Felix would have their way with me... regardless of what I did.

"Please..." I begged, desperate with panic. "Please, let me go..."

But they didn't. As soon as we entered the bedroom, Felix pushed me down on the bed and stood over me saying something to Victor in German. I didn't understand what, but Felix unbuckled his belt. I could see he wanted to take me immediately, even before Victor tied me up and started his fun and games.

Victor didn't look pleased at all, but Felix was paying him no heed. He was too horny to wait so he let his pants fall to the floor, and as he did, his erect penis stuck out of his boxer shorts. He wanted to take off his pants so he bent over to kick off his shoes. That was when I tried to sit up. But that didn't please Felix at all, so he pushed me back down on the bed. Once his shoes and pants were off, he held me down, spreading my legs and touching my pussy.

I squirmed and tried to close my legs but he wouldn't let me. "Let me go..." I cried hysterically. "I don't want you to touch me..."

That made Victor so furious he grabbed my arms and held me down on the bed while Felix forced my legs wider apart. But when Felix touched my pussy again, he found her dry and closed tight as a clam.

"Gleitcreme," Felix growled and motioned to Victor for some lube as I squirmed, still trying to get away. Victor let go of me to get the lube and I struggled again to sit up. He dropped the key to the storage room on the night table and pushed me down on the bed again.

"Stop, Victor, please!" I begged. "Please…! I don't want to… this is rape, God's sake…!"

Hearing me say that only enraged him more so he tossed the lube over to Felix and held me down vehemently, saying, "Rachel, if you don't stop this nonsense, I promise you, you'll never see Albert again. I promise."

I started to cry and both men laughed.

Felix squirted some lube out of the tube and rubbed it on my pussy, grunting with delight. Then he stuck his fat fingers up me, which my little pussy didn't like at all. I squirmed some more and cried out, which only made him laugh more.

Victor was getting aroused now too, even though he didn't seem very pleased at having Felix manhandle me like that. That was when he let go of my arms and stood up, opening his pants so his erect penis was positioned near my head. I watched it pulse and thought he was going to put it in my mouth, but he didn't. Instead he sat down beside me again, and began caressing my breasts. His touch was gentle at first, but then he pinched my nipples hard the way he thought I liked it. But I didn't and I struggled against his touch.

Oh God, help me! I thought, but there was nothing I could do. Not against Victor, not against these two men together. Not… I felt more hot tears in my eyes and closed them hard. They were both going to fuck me and fuck me hard. There was no getting away from what was happening…

Felix removed his fingers from my pussy and pulled me toward the edge of the bed so he could enter me standing while Victor was still holding my nipples tightly, trying to arouse me. That was when I felt Felix enter me and remembered the thickness of his penis as he drove it into me. He was wider than most men, stocky even there. He held on to my waist and began thrusting himself in and out, in and out; I cried out in pain. That turned Victor on so much he let go of my nipples and stood up so he could put his penis in my mouth.

"Take me in your mouth, Rachel," he commanded. When I didn't immediately do as he said, he grabbed my hair, pulling my head back. I cried out. That seemed to really excite Felix, who thrust himself even more forcefully into me.

I opened my mouth and felt Victor's pulsing penis almost choking me. Victor was holding my arms above my head so I couldn't move, Felix was holding my hips and thrusting himself into me; Victor was breathing hard, really excited now. I was spread eagle and completely open now... and I felt myself dissolving and disappearing into the blackness and blankness of the two men pounding into me, one in my pussy, the other in my mouth.

All I wanted to do was disappear and I was sure I was... disappearing...

Suddenly there was no longer any me; only a body; only a wave of sensation, only a...

That was when I felt myself slipping away... in a swoon... into the nothingness... because there was nothing I could do... nothing... but give up... so I did... and then, all of a sudden, I found myself drifting... drifting somewhere else... floating somewhere outside of my body... looking down at the carnal act that was unfolding on the bed below where Felix and Victor were fucking the living daylights out of me. It all seemed so gross... but I felt nothing... it was as if I was watching from afar and it was so very peaceful there where I was... floating quietly, up above the bed below, unconcerned, unafraid, free... feeling so peaceful that I never wanted to go back... never... ever... ever... I just wanted to stay there, floating... floating...

Aaahhh...

But it was not to be... no... because Victor suddenly withdrew his pulsing penis from my mouth and that snapped me back to reality… and right back into my body.

It was a rude awakening.

Startled by the physicality of my own body again, and by the grossness of what was happening to me, I opened my eyes and looked up. Victor had a strange look of dismay on his face as he turned and regarded Felix who was holding my waist as he neared his climax. Victor slid down and began kissing me on the face; I closed my eyes. He was holding my breasts gently and whispering in my ear, "Oh Rachel, I'm sorry I did this… so sorry… I didn't realize what I was doing; I should have never let Felix have you like this. Please forgive me, look at me, look at me! Open your eyes…"

He let go of my breasts and held my face in his hands. Felix was groaning and growling, finding his rhythm at last, but Victor kept holding my face tight in his hands.

"Rachel, look at me. Look at me."

I opened my eyes and gazed into his intense, smoldering gaze and realized Victor was madly jealous that Felix was fucking me. "You are mine, Rachel. Only mine! I'll never let you go…"

Now he was excited too, so he got up and rammed his pulsing penis into my mouth again. I closed my eyes, hoping against hope that I could escape my body again… but it was not to be… no… not this time… there was no more escaping… so I watched the tide take me as Felix came thundering to his climax in me – and Victor, groaning loudly, climaxed in my mouth too. I swallowed the accursed man's cum and heard them both, panting hard.

Victor slowly removed his penis from my mouth.

Felix was still inside me, still panting.

I didn't dare open my eyes, instead I prayed. Prayed for a miracle, prayed for release from this nightmare.

Felix slowly withdrew his penis from my aching pussy.

Then it was quiet, very quiet.

My eyes were still closed, but I heard Victor pull up his pants and walk over to Felix and pat him on the back.

"Come, let's go have a drink," Victor said slowly.

I heard Felix grunt and pull up his pants.

I opened my eyes, just slightly, and saw Victor putting his arm around Felix's shoulder as if they were best buddies.

I lay perfectly still, not daring to breathe. Then in a moment of sudden insight, I realized that Victor, in his mad jealousy, wanted to get Felix away from me.

Felix wiped his brow and grunted with satisfaction.

And with that, Victor led Felix out of the room.

The moment the door closed, I sat up and looked around the room. They were gone and Victor hadn't tied me up.

I breathed a long sigh of relief... then I thought...

Now is my chance to escape.

Now is my chance!

I jumped up and made straight for the window, ready to climb out and run.

I undid the latch, softly, softly.

I started to open it carefully, not wanting to make a sound.

But then I stopped short.

What about Claudia? I can't just leave her here, locked in the storage room. Who knows what they might do to her...

My heart was thumping in my chest. There wasn't a minute to lose. Who knew when those two maniacs would come back for more?

Then I thought about trying to find Claudia.

I don't even know where she is...

There's no time to lose!

I have to find her... but, oh God, but what if they hear me? Discover me?

I didn't even know where the storage room was.

I can't just leave her...

In a split second, I made my decision and turned back from the window. I picked up the little key on the night table and tiptoed over to the door.

I held my breath and opened it slowly. Ever so slowly. Praying it wouldn't squeak.

Oh God, what if they hear me?

I felt the adrenaline coursing through my body. My heart thumped in my chest.

I peeked out into the hallway. Down at the one end, the door to the lounge was slightly open and I could hear Victor and Felix laughing and talking.

Where is the storage room? I thought. *Where??*

I didn't have a clue.

I knew the two doors after the room I was in towards the lounge where they were sitting led to the Jacuzzi room and to another bedroom, which meant the storage room had to be the other way. I turned and tiptoed down the hall, naked except for the black corset. On my way, I gently tried each door I passed. The first two opened easily and led to other bedrooms, but the third was locked! As I tried the knob, I heard movement inside.

This must be where Claudia is!

I stuck the key in the lock and gently opened the door. Claudia jumped up as I did and embraced me.

"Shhhh!" I hissed putting my finger to my lips.

"Hurry! We've got to get out of here before they come back... is there another way out?" I cried. There was no time to explain.

"There's a back door. Follow me," she whispered.

"Quietly," I cried, terrified we'd be discovered.

We tiptoed down the hall, Claudia leading the way, me following. She turned down a small passageway which ended in a door to the lower garden.

"Quiet!" I hissed again.

She opened the door carefully and we could hear the sea. We slipped out silently without closing the door and ran towards the house as fast as we could.

"Get your passports, keys and money," Claudia cried as we

entered the house. "I've got to get the recordings. Meet you at the car in a jiffy! Hurry!" She headed downstairs to her room.

I stormed up the stairs to our bedroom, shaking all over. I pulled on some jeans and a sweatshirt and slipped into my Converse shoes. I grabbed my leather jacket and big shoulder bag and made sure I had my phone, credit cards and car keys. Then I rummaged through the drawer with my private papers looking for our passports. *Where are they?*

I saw the deed to the Soho loft – I grabbed it and stuffed it and the keys to the loft into my bag.

My heart was pounding my chest.

Where are our passports? Our passports! I must have them…

The adrenaline was coursing through my body.

It wouldn't be long before Victor discovered I was gone!

Here they are!

I sighed with relief and stuffed the three passports into my bag and ran down the stairs and out to the car. Claudia wasn't there.

I got in and put the keys in the ignition, ready to go.

Claudia! Come on Claudia! Where are you?

I felt the sweat trickling down under my arms…

I pounded on the steering wheel in frustration.

Where are you?

I knew we couldn't wait much longer.

Claudia, Claudia! Come on!

Time was running out.

Claudia! Where are you?

From where I sat, I could see down the slope to the annex and guest house below. The lights were shining brightly in the lounge where Victor and Felix were sitting, but suddenly they flickered off. That meant they were going back to the bedroom to find me!

I had to go now or it would be too late!

There wasn't a moment to lose.

Claudia where are you?

I turned on the ignition and at that very moment, the car door burst open and Claudia jumped in with a big bag over her shoulder, holding her computer to her breast. She was panting.

"Drive!" she cried.

I had to turn the car around so I backed up and started turning.

At that very moment, we heard the sound of Victor shouting on the slope below.

"What the hell is going on?" he yelled at the top of his lungs. And then, when he realized what was happening, he hollered, "Stop! Stop, Rachel! Or I won't pay the ransom for Albert! Stop or you'll be sorry!"

"Drive!" Claudia cried. "Don't listen to that idiot! Just drive!"

"He'll die because of you!" Victor was hollering as he ran up the slope. "He will!" He was almost up to the car.

"Don't listen to that idiot, Rachel!!" cried Claudia. "Just drive for God's sake!"

I took a deep breath and stepped on the gas. We sped out of the driveway.

"Rachel!" I heard Victor bellowing behind us. "Albert is a dead man… I promise you! I promise you!"

I turned onto the street and zoomed away.

We were free.

We were speeding down the open road on our way to Nice. It was almost midnight so there was very little traffic. I was going fast because I wanted to get as far away from Cap Ferrat as fast as I could. And I wanted to get my children as quick as I could and get away from the Riviera.

All of a sudden I felt really clear and focused.

And calm.

The path before me was clear.

I knew what I had to do.

I would take my kids and fly home. Back to New York. Right

away. Now.

"Suddenly you don't seem very upset about Victor's threat not to pay the ransom money..." Claudia said slowly after she'd settled down a bit.

"No," I replied, "I'm not. Because now I know it's not true."

"What do you mean, it's not true? How do you know that?"

"Because I spoke to Prince Abdul today," I replied softly.

"You did what... Why, Rachel... why didn't you tell me... "

When I didn't reply immediately she continued, "Rachel... what happened? When did he call? Why didn't you tell me?"

"It was right before I came down to the annex tonight so I didn't have a chance and then when I got there I was afraid Victor would turn up and hear..."

"Well, what happened?"

"Well, I'd been lying on my bed, thinking about what was about to happen and I was feeling absolutely miserable, Claudia... because I simply couldn't see a way out... All I wanted to do was run and hide but you'd convinced me that I couldn't because of the children... and that's when my phone rang. There was no caller ID so I almost didn't answer, but then for some reason I did. Thank God for that. When I answered, I heard a voice I didn't recognize saying 'Is this Rachel Somers?' My heart skipped a beat when I heard the accent because my first thought was that it was one of Albert's kidnappers trying to contact me. So I said, 'Yes, this is Rachel Somers' and then the man simply said 'My name is Prince Abdul'. I was so surprised I just blurted out... 'Prince Abdul... why, I've been trying to figure out how to get in touch with you for so long. Thank God you called.' So he was pretty surprised by my reaction – to say the least."

"Well, what did he say? Did you ask him?"

"Of course, and he said there was no truth whatsoever to what Victor has been saying. It turns out the Prince hasn't even spoken to Victor in months."

"Scumbag!" cried Claudia. "Oh, how I hate that man!"

"Yeah, me too," I said heatedly.

"I'd like nothing better than to rip his balls off!" Claudia hissed vehemently. I had to laugh because she said it with such passion – and this was the woman I not long ago had called the Ice Queen.

"You sound awfully jolly for someone's who's just been fucked back, front and sideways by two of the biggest sleazebags on earth."

"Yeah… well… maybe…" I said, considering her words. Because there was some truth to what she said. But in fact, I did feel rather jolly. I didn't quite know how to explain the strange sense of elation I was feeling.

So I was silent for a while and then I tried, "I don't know quite how to explain it to you, Claudia… but… it's just… well, now I'm free. I mean I really am… free. And I know what I'm going to do… and I also know that Albert's fate is not in my hands and not in the hands of that scumbag Victor either… His fate is in the hands of God… and it's just… I mean…. there's nothing more I can do to help Albert except pray for him and believe that God is looking after him. I can't help him by suffering any more. I just can't… And I know he wouldn't want me to either… so I just have to let it go… that's the best I can do… for Albert and for me and for the children…"

We drove for a while in silence while Claudia digested what I'd just said.

"What else did the Prince say? Why did he call you?"

"He said he was calling because he wanted to tell me he was doing everything in his power to try and track Albert's kidnappers down. It seems he's very fond of Albert… So that's why he called actually. Just to tell me he was working through his channels to see if he could find out anything."

"Well, that's good," replied Claudia. "A Saudi Prince like him must have many good connections in the Middle East."

"Yes, that's exactly what I thought. He said he'd spoken to

Jacques Durand at the Foreign Ministry so he knew they'd hit a brick wall and had pretty much given up... which was also why he wanted me to know he hadn't given up and wasn't going to give up. I cried when he said that. He gave me hope again..."

PART IV

ALBERT'S STORY CONTINUES

Albert had lost all trace of time; it had been so many months now. But suddenly he was aware of the sound of gunfire outside – and people shouting. It was all in Arabic so he didn't understand what they were saying, but at least he was wide awake again. The sound of gunfire had aroused him from his daze. It sounded like there was a small battle going on right outside his door. The shouting, the screaming, and the sound of machine guns; it all seemed to move closer and then it moved away again.

He was tied up so he couldn't move from the mattress he was sitting on, or stand up so he could try to look out the window. But now he remembered; they had moved him again – for the umpteenth time from God knows where to Gods know where again. It was always the same routine when they moved him, the injection, the blackout, and then the slow awakening again, somewhere – God only knew where. Every time he woke up, it was with the same aching head and feeling of nausea. Sometimes he wondered how much more of this his body could take. But he always tried to push the thought from his mind – and think of something pleasant, think of some little thing that pleased him – because he knew it was important to focus on something that made him want to stay alive and keep on living. But it wasn't always easy.

And today had been no exception.

The rottenness of it all made him feel like reeling.

Things seemed to fade in and out of his consciousness.

But there was gunfire again – awakening him from the cloud of confusion that so often enveloped him. He was having difficulty keeping track of time. He wasn't even sure anymore how long he had been in captivity.

He looked around the dingy room. He could see he was in a

traditional Arabic dwelling because the walls were made of sun-dried brick and clay. There were a few mattresses on the floor which was covered with palm leaf matting and a few goat-hair rugs. The tiny windows were shuttered shut to keep the heat and sun out.

He knew he was in Yemen.

Or at least that was what Rafiq told him in one of his more lucid moments. He had been retching after waking up from another injection and Rafiq must have taken pity on him. Rafiq was the only one of his captors who spoke a little English. And it was just after another one of their trips in the white van they used to move him when Rafiq said they were now in Yemen. It didn't make all that much difference to him where he was, but he knew somewhere in the corner of his mind that it was an important detail which he should keep track of, especially if he ever was going to get out of this alive.

Yemen. Yemen? Now why is this important?

The room faded in and out.

Oh yes, the gunfire outside. Yemen was in a terrible state of turmoil; that was something he did remember. Rival clans, Islamic militant groups and al-Qaeda all battling each other for supremacy; the country was failing apart. In chaos.

Then he remembered that when Rafiq told him they were in Yemen, the other two had punched Rafiq and shouted at him furiously. Rafiq was young, just a kid, Albert remembered thinking. He couldn't have been more than twenty. But after his slight kindness to Albert, he disappeared. He was gone. Simply gone. Albert wondered what had happened to him. Did they kill him for talking to Albert, or did they just send him on another mission?

It didn't bear thinking about.

But then what did?

As the gunfire faded into the distance, Albert slumped down on the dirty mattress again and dozed off. He was weak and exhausted after months in captivity, lack of food and exercise, combined with the ketamine injections and the sheer terror of his daily existence, if that's what it could be called.

All Albert knew was the endless tedium of being tied up with nothing to do or read. Then there was the occasional good day when he was not tied up but locked in a room instead. When that happened, he felt like celebrating because at least he could move around a little and try to exercise. But it didn't happen often and he was getting weaker and weaker. He knew he'd lost a lot of weight and sometimes he also thought he had a fever, but he tried not to think about it.

When they kept him in one place long enough for him to become a little more lucid, he found himself longing for a shave and a shower and clean clothes and something decent to eat. Those were things he could think about, but the real things he longed for – like freedom and Rachel and his daughter and his life – simply didn't bear thinking about. It was just too painful. So he didn't allow himself to go there in his mind. He was afraid it would drive him mad if he did... so instead he tried to focus on being present in the moment and finding something, anything, to occupy his mind. He told himself things like... *well this is pretty much the same as going to a Zen monastery for a six-month meditation retreat.* So he'd focus on his breathing or else try to pick something simple to focus on – like the light streaming through the crack in the shutter and how it filtered down to the dirty floor and illuminated it like fairy dust.

Like fairy dust... he was almost gone again... delirious almost...

The light flickered... or was it the fairy dust...

The sound of gunfire woke him up again from his daze. It was close by, so close that he knew the gun battle was raging all around him.

What was going on?

Would he get killed in the crossfire?

He felt woozy – It was only hours before that he'd awoken again from another ketamine injection, feeling disoriented and nauseous.

Two of his captors came charging into the room; they didn't look at him. The taller one opened the shutters and began shooting out into the street. The other was fumbling with a mobile phone, apparently they were trying to get in touch with someone. A minute later, the tall one shouted and they both charged out the door again, slamming it behind them.

Albert heard the gunfire move further down the street.

He struggled again with the rope holding him down because he wanted to stand up and look out the little window now that the shutters were open. But he couldn't move enough to do it so he slumped back down on the mattress in despair. He sensed nightfall was approaching.

He felt nauseous.

Quiet descended.

A tear trickled down his dirty cheek.

Much later in the dead of night, two women in black Niqabs woke him up. He was disoriented, confused; he didn't know where he was.

Where am I?

He looked from one covered figure to the other.

What's going on?

He struggled to wake up.

"Shhh…" They whispered emphatically and put their fingers to where their lips were behind the black veils.

They were untying him and struggling to get him up from the mattress.

He wasn't sure if they were friend or foe.

"What's going on?" he said out loud.

"Shhh… " The shorter of the two hissed at him. "Hurry… must hurry…" her English was difficult to understand.

"Come!" she hissed again.

He made an effort to get to his feet, but it was difficult.

The room seemed to turn. He thought he would vomit or pass out, but he struggled to get up.

When he was standing, the two women covered him quickly with a black Niqab, identical to the ones they were wearing.

"Come," the little one hissed again, "or you die."

He struggled to walk, but almost couldn't, he was so weak.

The women put his arms around each of their shoulders for support and led him carefully towards the door.

"Shhh...." The little one hissed again, "or we... die."

When she said that, he understood they were trying to help him.

He held his breath as they carefully opened the door and glided into the dark night.

It was pitch black outside.

There wasn't a sound anywhere.

It was the dead of night.

They glided down a nearby alleyway which seemed to lead through a maze of walled-in courtyards. The dirt floor of the alleyway was smooth enough but Albert was so weak he was afraid he would trip and stumble and awaken sleeping dogs behind the walls. But somehow he kept moving without stumbling. He leaned heavily on the two women and felt their bodies trembling as they tried to support him.

Fortunately for him, they didn't have far to go.

Not more than two or three hundred meters down the alleyway, a door opened and they entered a courtyard. Once inside, he felt the women breathe easier and soon they entered one of the dwellings situated further down the property. Someone was obviously waiting for them because the door opened immediately, and inside several more women completely covered in black Niqabs were waiting for them. They spoke softly in hushed voices with one another and led him to a small room with a mattress on the floor. They removed the Niqab he was wearing and let him down gently onto the mattress where he passed out.

He did not know for sure if it was true or not, but it seemed to him that there was gunfire in the early hours of the morning and the sound of men shouting at the women outside his room. But he was too weak and delirious to be sure if it was actually happening or if it was just a fever dream. And besides, there was nothing he could do about it anyway so he just succumbed to the furnace-like feeling in his body and the fever he'd been battling for days, and slipped back into the blessed oblivion of sleep.

That was when he began seeing visions of Rachel... or so he thought... floating on her back in the blue water of his swimming pool outside his house on Cap Ferrat. She was laughing and smiling at him with those incredible green eyes of hers...

Her name was Safa, the one who was nursing him. She was the little one who had first spoken to him when they came to his rescue. Gently she fed him; gently she wiped his feverish forehead. Gently. Sometimes he could almost focus on her. But many days were to pass before the fever broke and the delirium passed. He remembered her giving him medicine and making him drink, but much more than that he didn't remember. Until one morning he awoke and was aware of the silence – and of the young woman sitting by his side on the floor, watching him. She was unveiled and he saw she was a slight, slip of a woman with raven black hair and big black eyes. She couldn't have been more than twenty-seven or twenty-eight.

She smiled slowly when she saw he was awake and said in broken English, "Me... Safa. You feel... better?"

He turned her question over in his mind and then he said slowly, "Yes... a little."

She gave him a glass of water.

He drank hungrily. He was so thirsty.

She gave him another glass and he drank more.

Then he slept again.

Next time he woke, she asked him, "Who are you?"

It was an effort to talk, but he managed to say, "My name is Albert. Albert Giovanni."

He felt himself slipping away but she shook his arm. "Why... are you... so important?"

He forced himself to focus. That was when he realized the women who saved him didn't even know who he was.

"Why... they look for you?"

When he didn't answer, she continued. "They look in... all houses... here... everywhere... look for you... even houses for women like this house... to find you."

He struggled to answer even though he felt himself succumbing to the fever again. "I've very rich and they've asked for a lot of money for my release."

And with that he was gone again.

Several days later when he was able to sit up and eat a little, Safa asked him again, "You say you... you are... Albert... Albert Giovanni... these men want money... money for you... you say. How much?" When she said that, he realized that these women had just helped him because they knew he was a hostage, an innocent man being held unjustly by one of the fanatical militant groups who were terrorizing Yemen. More than that they did not know.

Nor did they realize how dangerous it was for them to be hiding him.

When he had eaten a little more of the thin gruel she was feeding him, he replied slowly, "Five million Euros."

"Five million..." she gasped in surprise.

"Yes," he said, "five million Euros..."

"You must be..." she said slowly.

"Yes, I am," he replied softly. "How long have I been here?"

"Ten days," she said, holding up her fingers.

He knew he shouldn't, he knew it was not permitted in traditional Arabic relations between men and women who were not related, but he was so moved by her bravery that he reached out for her hand anyway. He was surprised when she let him take it.

"You saved my life," he said, patting her hand gently. "How can I ever thank you?"

When she didn't answer, he rubbed his beard and continued. "I really need a wash and a shave."

That was the first time he saw her smile.

But many more days were to pass before he was strong enough to get up. Safa had nursed him patiently through those first critical ten days, especially because he was too weak to do anything for himself. The only help she had was the three other women who looked in on him when she was away. He didn't know their names, but he understood that besides being shy about having a man, a foreigner and a Westerner, in their very private women's quarters to look after, they didn't speak or understand English.

But slowly, slowly as he became more lucid, he began to contemplate his situation and his next move. How was he ever going to get out of there to safety without getting discovered by his abductors, and without endangering the lives of these very brave women?

Two days later, Safa brought him a newspaper, The International Herald Tribune. The first thing he looked at was the date. September tenth it said.

When he pointed at the date, Safa said, "Old newspaper... maybe two weeks old..."

But he didn't care. Now he knew how long he'd been held hostage. He was abducted in late December the year before, outside his hotel in Amman.

"It's almost ten months since I was kidnapped, Safa," was all he could say. "Ten months..."

Her eyes were bright with tears.

A few days later, he was finally able to get up and wash himself on his own and shave. He felt it was a minor miracle and his heart nearly burst with gratitude. When Safa came to see him later that afternoon she got a shock – she hadn't realized what a handsome man she'd rescued.

Shyly she gave him the little package she'd brought with her and shyly he opened it. Inside the brown paper was a brand new white shirt.A brand new, clean white, western-style shirt.

"Oh, Safa," he cried in delight. "Never have I been so delighted to receive a shirt in my whole life."

So they became fast friends, and during her daily visits, he slowly learned more of her story and she more of his. Now that he was regaining his strength, he was starting to wonder about things.

Safa had gone to university and was now one of the few women in Yemen who was interning to be a doctor. When he heard this, he exclaimed teasingly, "So that's how you knew what to do with me."

"Yes," she exclaimed and smiled shyly, "I get antibiotics from doctor... at hospital. I work there... at hospital ... I am... intern. He tells me what to do. You...so ill... I must ask someone..."

It turned out she was quite a feisty little woman because besides rescuing hostages in her free time, she was also an active supporter of the women's freedom movement "Women Journalists Without Chains". The group, which was founded by Yemeni human rights activist and Nobel Prize winner, Tawakul Karman, was often on the front line of the battle for change in Yemen. It also turned out that Safa was unmarried, which was unusual for a woman her age in Yemen. But this, she said, was because she had refused to marry when she was younger and now she was a campaigner against child marriage.

"Lucky me... now everyone... my whole family... thinks me

too old… to be married," she said laughingly."Never, ever married!" She seemed truly relieved at the prospect, so relieved that Albert couldn't help but take her hand again. He was growing truly fond of her and she of him.

They sat like that for a while in silence.

Then he said, "I've been wondering for a while – how did you discover I was being held hostage down the street?"

"Oh… it was… accident," she said, still struggling to find the right words even though her English was improving fast, thanks to their daily talks. "Alaa… you know, my friend, Alaa… well, her brother… her little brother, Ibrahim. He is seven only. He playing… outside house… you inside. He heard these men talk. Ibrahim told Alaa. At first she laughed, but then she tells me. When the gun battle starts on the street, I wonder what about man inside. After the guns stop, I think… I must go and see… so in the nighttime, we go… looking… "

They were silent for a while and then Albert said what they were both thinking, "How are we ever going to get me out of here… without me being recaptured and without endangering you and the other women for hiding me?"

Part V

New York

Life suddenly seemed really slow for me. As if everything had become very quiet.

Because it was.

I was back in New York with my children, living in our loft in Soho, the one Albert had given me just before he left for Jordan. And strange as it may seem, even if we were in the middle of a big city – everything was so very quiet. Which meant I had a chance to think – and feel again.

And think and feel again I did.

And it was painful, oh so painful.

I missed Albert terribly.

Often I'd wake up in the middle of the night in a sweat with my heart crying out – *Albert, Albert... where are you?*

Where are you?

What's happened to you, what, what, what?

Are you dead or alive?

But there was no answer – none whatsoever – only silence.

So I didn't know what to think, I simply couldn't know.

But somehow, it didn't feel like he was dead... it just didn't.

Somehow I felt, when I really let myself feel, that I would feel it, know it, if he was dead.

But I didn't dare believe that either.

So I just didn't know.

And there was... only silence... only that terrible, empty silence.

It was mid-September when I fled from the house on Cap Ferrat and now it was almost the end of October and I was getting more and more restless. I just didn't know what to do with myself; I was so agitated, upset, uneasy all the time, and couldn't find peace anywhere. My plan was to go back to school and study psychology at New York University, but the semester had already begun so I couldn't start until the next term. So I spent most of my time with my children, mothering them, playing with them, caring for them, and loving them. Little Isabella was now one and a half years old – and she was a tiny miracle with her curly, jet black hair and dark flashing eyes as she toddled around. She looked just like her father and was my little bundle of joy in the midst of my sorrow.And her big brother, Daniel, who was now six, adored her almost as much as I did.

Moreover there was Isabel, my mother, who was such an incredible support and comfort to me. In fact, being able to spend time with her was, by far, the best thing about returning to New York, because she was really there for me. I could pour my heart out to her and share all my agony and distress – and she listened and understood. So the children and I visited her often at her house on Long Island, or she would come to the city and stay with us for a few days.

When she was in town, I'd let Amélie take the children out so my mother and I could have one of our many long talks. One of the things we discussed a lot was whether or not we should try to press charges against Victor Gandler for what he did to me. At first, I didn't dare tell my mother what really happened, but when she finally got the truth out of me, she was shocked and outraged – and wanted us to bring the man to justice. But the more we talked about it, the more she began to understand how difficult it would be to do. Victor would be a formidable opponent even if we did have Claudia's recording of the conversation where he blackmailed me. Unfortunately, the reality was, without Albert, we had no champion. Stefan – as much as I loved him – was not a powerful man like Albert or Victor. So how would we go about making our case?

Both my mother and I were too fragile at the moment for such an undertaking, so every time we discussed it, we'd both come to the same conclusion – that for the time being, we had to wait. We had to wait for a sign. Wait until we were both stronger. Wait to see if there would be news of Albert. Wait to see if… But oh, the waiting was almost intolerable and seemed to go on forever. Because there was no getting around the horror of what had happened – to Albert and to me – and there was no getting around the dreadful uncertainty of not knowing whether Albert was dead or alive.

So even though I'd been in New York for almost one and a half months and was beginning to settle into my new life, my unease and agitation didn't subside. In fact, it only seemed to get worse. I was feeling so shaky that my mother started talking about me getting some help and going to therapy to deal with the trauma I had suffered. And I was seriously considering doing so. But then one morning I woke up with a new idea, which surprised me. But the idea had come with such force and clarity, that I knew I had to consider it.

Consider going to the Buddhist monastery Albert sponsored in upstate New York to try meditating for a while. Maybe that would help me calm down and find some peace.

Yes, that was the idea.

Why not go and meditate?

I'd never done anything like that before, but for some reason, it just felt right. And the more I toyed with the idea, the more I felt I should give it a try. For some reason, I felt sure that Albert would want me to do it too.

In fact, as I lay in bed that morning, I remembered how he told me he went to Japan to meditate after I left Nice that fateful October because he was so distraught. He said that was what he learned to do when life became too much. He said it was difficult to do, especially when your mind was going crazy, but if you persisted in your meditation practice, sooner or later, you would calm down and find some peace. And if there was anything I needed at that point in time, it was some peace.

Peace. Oh, how it eluded me.

I was just such a bundle of nerves – in constant turmoil. I simply couldn't find release anywhere.

So right then and there, I made up my mind to go.

I'd already been to the monastery, so I knew the place. Albert took me there to meet his old sensei right before Isabella was born. I remembered it well; the spacious, old, wooden buildings and meditation hall, the lovely mountain air, and the profound feeling of peace that enveloped the place.

Maybe it will be good for me, I thought.

And since Amélie had come to America with me and the children, I could easily leave them with her and my mother for a couple of weeks. I knew that my mother would gladly have them stay with her at her house on Long Island.

So by the time I got out of bed that morning, I had decided to go. I began making the arrangements at once. Fortunately for me, the monastery was offering a three-week meditation retreat that was starting the very next week. And there was room for one more participant. I took that as an auspicious sign.

Two days into the retreat, I broke down.

The program was quite strict, even if it was open to beginners like me, with meditation sessions morning, afternoon and evening. Interspersed with intervals of nature walks, dharma talks, walking meditation, and working in the kitchen or around the monastery. There were twenty people in the group.

Anton Fraser, head of the monastery, led the program and gave the dharma talks. Sometimes he was present during the meditation sessions too, sitting with us.

I remembered him from the time I visited the monastery with Albert and he remembered me. He knew about Albert's abduction and treated me with the utmost kindness.

On the evening of the second day, during the evening meditation, I was suddenly and unexpectedly overwhelmed by an intense wave of sadness and grief. I was sitting there, trying to focus on my breathing, but simply couldn't because of a powerful, gut-wrenching cry that seemed to well up from within me. I began to sob hysterically as I sat there on the wooden floor on my meditation cushion.

It was as if I'd been hit by a tsunami of such intense anguish that after a few moments, I had to get up and run out of the building because the sobs were turning into a howl of anguish. So out I ran, sobbing, and for some reason, headed straight towards the thick cluster of trees on the other side of the wide grass lawn. But it was dark outside and I tripped over a rock and landed flat on my face on the cold ground, sobbing.

And in that blackness, on the cold, cold ground, I just lay there, writhing in agony.

A few moments later, I felt a gentle hand on my back and a kind voice saying, "It's okay, Rachel, it's okay… it's okay…"

Even though I heard the voice and the kindness in it, I didn't look up but just kept on sobbing uncontrollably.

My whole body was wracked with anguish.

But the hand didn't move. Instead it just kept resting gently but firmly on my back, as the storm raged within me.

Time passed and the hand stayed, waiting patiently for the raging storm to subside as I lay crumpled on ground, sobbing.

After a while I noticed it was cold out.

That was when I realized that the violent sobbing had subsided a bit and now I was just crying softly.

The gentle hand was still resting firmly on my back.

I turned my head and looked up.

It was Anton Fraser.

He didn't say anything, he was just there.

Another wave of sobs hit me and I convulsed again.

He stayed there, like a rock.

When the convulsion passed, I struggled to sit up only to discover I was shivering all over.

"I'm freezing," I cried, wiping my nose on my sleeve.

"Yes," he said quietly, "I can see that. How about we get you inside?"

He helped me up and brushed me off.

"Come," he said, "let's get you into a warm bed."

And with that, he led me to my room in the sleeping quarters. Fortunately I had my own private room so I wasn't sharing it with anyone. When we got there, he said, "Rachel, you get undressed and get into bed. I'm going to go get you some hot tea."

When he saw the look of terror on my face, he added softly, "Don't worry. I'll be back in two minutes. Now get undressed and get into bed. I want you to get warm."

It was almost November and the evenings were cold up in the mountains. He turned on the heater full blast and left to get some tea.

I did as he said.

Two minutes later, he returned with a thermos and two cups. I was in bed. He pulled up the only chair in the room next to the bed and poured the tea.

"Now drink this."

His kindness only made me cry more.

He didn't say a word; he just let me cry.

Time passed and the sobbing became less again.

"Thank you," I said, wiping my noise with one of the tissues he gave me.

"It's okay, Rachel," he said slowly, "I can imagine the hell you've been through."

"Yes…" I said slowly as the tears began to flow again, "and it still feels that way."

"Well, meditation does that, you know. I mean meditation does make us intensely aware of what's going on inside us. So it makes sense that you would feel it all so acutely now."

And with that, he let me settle into the silence of the room. Even though he didn't say it in so many words, he made it clear to me that he wasn't going to leave until I was ready to be on my own.

I sipped my tea and he picked up his cup and sipped his too.

I was glad for his company.

The next morning after breakfast, Anton took me to his office and asked me how I was doing.

"To be honest, I'm feeling pretty shaky," I replied truthfully.

"Yeah, that's what I figured. You know, I don't think it's a good idea for you to continue with the meditation retreat at the moment, Rachel; you're simply too vulnerable."

"It's true," I replied, relieved to hear his assessment of the situation. "I'm scared to death that if I go back to the meditation hall, I'll freak out again."

"There's a good chance you will," he said. "You probably don't know it, Rachel, but I'm a psychotherapist, so I have to say, I agree, you're not ready for such an intense meditation retreat. Not yet."

We sat in silence for a bit on his roomy couch.

"Are you saying I should go home? Do you think I should go back to New York?"

"Well, that's a possibility," he said, "if that's what feels right to you. But if you want to, you could stay on and you and I could meet every day for counseling sessions. That's what I do, so maybe I can help you get a little more clarity about how you are feeling. Then, if you begin to feel a little more stable, you can join in some of the sessions for a short meditation if you want."

"Oh, thank you, Anton," I exclaimed, liking him even more. "I feel like such a mess right now. Do you think you can help me?"

"Well, I don't know," he laughed, "but I can try."

When he said those words, I felt a great wave of relief wash over me because I didn't want to give up after just two days at the monastery and go back to New York. I knew there was something deeper going on here, even though I wasn't quite sure what it was.

"How can I ever thank you?"

"You don't have to. Albert is a good friend. We spent time together in Japan with our master Okumara Sensei, so we know each other well. Plus he's the patron of this place. So it's the least I can do."

So it was settled.

I was to stay on and start therapy with Anton that very afternoon. Besides that, we agreed that I could go walking in the woods around the monastery and help in the kitchen. And whenever I felt ready, I could join the meditation sessions for as long as I felt comfortable, even if, in the beginning, it was only for ten or fifteen minutes at a time. It was up to me.

During the first three days of my therapy sessions, we talked about Albert and his abduction and the grief, fear and uncertainty I was feeling.

"It's more than eleven months now since Albert was kidnapped," I said slowly on the third day. It felt like a terrible pressure on my chest.

"Yes, I know," replied Anton evenly.

Then finally, we talked about the possibility of him being dead.

"It was late June when the Foreign Ministry called and said they'd lost all contact with Albert's abductors and that I should prepare myself for the worst..."When I finally said those words out loud, I was overcome by all the grief and anguish again – just as I had been that night when I ran out of the evening meditation session.

"For all I know, he could be dead!" I wailed.

Anton didn't say anything but just let me cry.

In a way, it was a relief to finally be able say it out loud and to own my own grief.

After I cried for a long while, I started to realize that I hadn't allowed myself to feel what I been feeling up until then, mainly because of what had gone on with Victor Gandler – and then because I'd been distracted by my escape and moving to New York and the settling in.

But now, there was finally time to feel.

Then suddenly on the fifth day of our sessions, I found myself telling Anton what had happened with Victor. It felt like ripping my chest open to talk about it and the fact that I told Anton about it at all was as much a surprise to me as it was to him.

I didn't mean to tell him.

In fact, I don't think I meant to tell anyone, ever.

But it just came out.

Anton literally turned pale when he heard my story.

"But, Rachel," he cried, "that was rape!"

"Yes, I know," I said through my sobs. "But I thought I had to do it, in order to save Albert."

"You have to report this man to the police. He should go to jail."

"But it's complicated."

"Why is it complicated? Tell me! What's so complicated about the fact that he raped you, over and over again?"

So I tried. I tried to explain the situation and how it unfolded in all its dreadful detail. Victor's role in Albert's company, how powerful he was, the way he'd planned everything, the way he had manipulated me, and then when it came to the sex itself, I found myself holding my stomach in both shame and anger.

"But I'm so ashamed, Anton," I cried, sobbing violently. "Ashamed!"

He let me cry.

Then he asked softly, "Why are you ashamed, Rachel? Why? What did you do to be ashamed of? Tell me!"

The room was so quiet you could have heard a pin drop.

Finally, I said it so softly I almost couldn't hear my own words, "Because he said that if I didn't cooperate, he wouldn't pay the money. He wouldn't pay the five million Euros in ransom if I didn't cooperate. And by cooperate he meant… if I didn't let myself go and enjoy the sex…" and with that, when the words were finally out… I began to howl… howl!

"Don't you see, Anton? I had to enjoy it. Can't you see it? Can't you understand what I'm saying?" Now I was almost shouting. "I had to let myself go and behave like a common slut and enjoy having sex with this despicable man who I detested and who was raping me! I had to!"

When I'd said those words, I buckled over and wept uncontrollably.

Finally, I looked up and said softly, "And the worst part was, I did. I did let myself go and I did have orgasm, countless times with that wretched man. Oh God, help me!"

Anton just sat there and let me cry.

"And the most horrible part of all… is… that orgasm feels like orgasm, which is good, which is very good… even if it's bad… very bad."

When those words came out, I buried my head in shame.

The next day at my session with Anton, even more came out. It was like once the dam had broken, the floodwaters just came pouring forth and I had to tell him that what happened with Victor wasn't the first time in my life something like that had happened. I don't know why, but I just had to tell him. It was like a confession. I had to tell him everything – *everything* – as if I was seeking absolution or something. So I said it, I told him that this had happened to me before – with Howard. And even, in a way, with Felix during my very first stay in Nice. I had to tell him that I had orgasm with men who were abusing me and I liked it. I just did.

And that I felt so defective because of it, so sick and ashamed of myself.

I wept as I told him and when I was finished, the room was very quiet for a long, long time. I sat there, feeling acutely aware of my body and my heart pounding in my chest.

Anton just sat there and let me calm down. Finally, when my breathing began to return to normal, Anton said in a very soft voice. "Rachel, to begin with, you must understand how our bodies work. It's important to understand that physical sensations are physical sensations. By that I mean, our bodies are designed to respond to sexual stimulation with pleasure – no matter what the situation is or how the sexual stimulation comes about. And this means our bodies are designed to respond this way even if our minds are screaming something else. Do you understand what I'm saying?"

When I didn't reply, he continued, "What I'm saying is sexual pleasure is sexual pleasure regardless of the situation in which it is happening. That's the way our bodies are made. Our bodies feel, they don't think. So they respond automatically to sexual stimulation. And this can be very confusing when we are being abused because even if we hate the situation we are in, when the sexual pleasure occurs, it still feels good. And it feels good even if we hate the person involved because it's just not humanly possible to dislike the pleasure itself. It doesn't work like that."

He paused for a while to let his words sink in.

Then he went on, "Why do you think so many incest victims feel such terrible shame about what happened to them? Even if they didn't do anything wrong, even if they were the victims of abuse, they often struggle with intense guilt and shame because the sex felt good even if they knew it was wrong when it was happening. Or if they were very young children when the incest took place and they later come to understand that they were being abused and that it was terribly wrong, many still felt pleasure when it happened. And this is so confusing because victims of incest, and even rape in a case like yours, can't make their intellectual understanding of the situation match what they actually felt.

"So not only is it confusing, it is the source of so much shame for so many people. And this is exactly what's happened to you, Rachel. It's what you've experienced – it's exactly the same thing. You were in a situation where you were forced to do something despicable – to do something you didn't want to do with someone you despised – and then you felt pleasure. It's a terrible burden to carry around, Rachel. It really is!"

Anton was pacing the room now and he paused for a few moments to look out the window at the beautiful autumn colors all around us.

Then he turned back to me and continued, "So please, Rachel, you must stop beating yourself up for what happened. It wasn't your fault and you didn't do anything wrong.

"And this doesn't mean you should forgive Victor or that you shouldn't press charges against him. That's not what I'm saying. But it's important for you to stop beating yourself up for what happened. It was not your fault. Do you understand? That's why it's so important for you to understand that it was impossible for you not to feel pleasure once you were aroused in that way.

"It's important to remember that the sexual drive is the most powerful drive of all. And because of that, when we human beings become aroused, there is very little our intellect or will power can do to stop this powerful urge for pleasure and orgasm and release... Why do you think everyone on this planet is so occupied with sex?"

He sat down again and looked at me intently as I tried to digest what he was saying. Then I asked in a whisper, "So... is this also what's happening in abusive relationships? Is it the same confusion?"

"Yes," he replied, "it is often the same confusion when it happens in an abusive relationship. Often the woman can't understand how she can go back to the abuser, but then when she does, the sex feels so good. So she thinks it must be love which makes it all so very confusing."

"Yes, I know..." I whispered. "I was so afraid of my ex-husband… and yet I stayed with him for so long…" I bowed my head in shame, thinking of my relationship with Jan.

"There's so much drama in abusive relationships," said Anton softly. "And what often happens is after all the drama, an abusive man will apologize to his victim and say it will never happen again and then there's the great make-up sex, which despite all that went on before… is so fantastic. And because the make-up sex is so fantastic, the woman mistakenly believes this must be a sign that it's true love. It must be true love because it feels so good. What else could it be?

"But the reality is, it's not true love and it has nothing to do with true love. True love is a completely different vibrational frequency characterized by deep respect and an unconditional acceptance of each person's right to be who they are, coupled with the understanding that each person is responsible for his or her own life choices and happiness. True love has nothing to do with expecting other people to sacrifice their own integrity and think, act, or behave to please the other person."

We sat in silence for a while and I was grateful that Anton gave me time to absorb what he was saying.

Talking to him gave me a lot to think about – and I realized I had a lot to learn.

Finally, he cleared his throat and said, "Nothing satisfies like sex. Nothing completes like sex. Nothing releases like sex. Nothing can compete with the ecstasy and bliss one experiences during the sexual encounter… except maybe enlightenment."

Everyday after my afternoon session with Anton, I would go for a walk in the woods around the monastery. It was early November so the leaves had turned and the forest was a symphony of reds and golds. The weather was lovely and rather warm for the time of year, so I liked to sit under an amazing old oak tree I discovered not far from the monastery. There was lovely soft grass around the old tree and I loved sitting with my back against it and letting myself feel and contemplate all the things that came up in my sessions with Anton.

He was a really good therapist – kind and funny and wise. What I liked the most about him was he gave me new ways of looking at things and a new understanding of what I was going through. He also gave me the time and space to find myself in the midst of all the turmoil I was experiencing. So for the first time in a very long time, I was beginning to feel a little bit calmer and a little bit more peaceful inside.

The other thing I liked about our sessions was that sometimes Anton would share a little of his own story with me. One day, he surprised me by saying that the reason he knew so much about sex and how powerful the energy of it was – was because before he became a Buddhist, he'd been a sex addict.

"Seriously?" I cried when he told me that because I really didn't understand what he meant. "What's a sex addict?"

"Well," he replied, "when I was in my early twenties, I simply couldn't make it through the day without having orgasm at least several times a day – and preferably with different women. Nothing turned me on more than managing to have sex with one or more beautiful women everyday."

I laughed out loud when he said that.

In fact, we both laughed out loud.

"Well, it's good to know I'm not the only one who's so hung up on sex," I said smiling. Just the thought of him being so hooked on sex and having sex with as many women as he could, made me feel a little more normal.

Then one day, after I'd been at the monastery for about eight days, Anton turned up while I was sitting under the oak tree, enjoying the sun dancing on the colorful leaves all around me.

I smiled when I saw him approaching.

"May I join you?" he said.

"Why, of course."

He sat down beside me and leaned up again the old tree too.

We sat for a while in silence, enjoying the peaceful afternoon and the sun.

He was the first to break the silence.

"Rachel," he said, "there's something I have to tell you."

I turned pale when he said those words and looked at him in dismay. "You've heard something about Albert?" I cried. People attending the retreat had to deliver their phones at the office when starting the retreat, so no one could call me directly.

"No, no. Easy now, easy," he said, taking my hand. "It's nothing like that."

"Oh, you scared me," I said, taking a deep breath and leaning back against the tree. "Then what is it?"

He was still holding my hand, looking at it and stroking it gently. It was the first time I really noticed the tattoo on his left hand.

"Rachel, I don't know how to say this… but…"

"Say what?"

"Well, it's like this…" he continued hesitantly, "I… I think about you a lot, Rachel…"

"What?" I asked, not understanding what he was saying.

"It's just… well…" he hesitated again.

"Just what?" I said, wondering what he was driving at. I gently pulled my hand away from his and put it in my pocket.

He sighed and looked up at the sky. "I know I shouldn't, Rachel, I know it's all wrong, but … there's just something about you… and… well… I can't get you out of my mind."

I turned and looked at him in surprise.

He had a look on his face I hadn't seen before, a hungry look. I was taken aback.

What was going on? Was Anton falling for me?

I'd been so wrapped up in my own distress that the thought had never occurred to me.

But now it was there.

And now that he'd said it, now that he'd articulated what was going on with him, I knew in my heart that the feeling had been there for a while, even though I never really registered it consciously before now.

"Oh, Anton..." I started to say, but stopped because I remembered how he told me he once had been addicted to women and sex.

Was that what was going on?

Had all our conversations about sex somehow triggered his old addiction?

I was watching the light on the trees. The beautiful, flickering light...

"But you're my therapist," I said softly.

"Yes, I know, I know," he said. "I know I am and I know that I'm not supposed to have these kinds of feelings for you... but the reality is I do."

When I didn't say more, he went on, "I just can't get you out of my head, Rachel! And God knows I've tried. I've tried to stop thinking about you, tried not to feel like this. But the reality is... all I want to do is..." but he didn't finish his sentence.

We sat in silence for a while.

"You told me once..." but I didn't finish my sentence either because he did.

"Yes," he said, "I did. I told you how I'd been addicted to sex when I was younger. And how I recovered. But now it's as if... it's been awakened in me again."

I turned and looked into his handsome face. He had high cheekbones and strong angular features. But all I could see was his torment.

He started to lean towards me.

But just at that moment, as he began leaning towards my lips, someone came bursting out of the forest.

We both turned to see who it was. To our surprise, it was Denise Walker, head of the monastery kitchen and a dedicated Buddhist practitioner, and she was marching straight towards us.

Anton jumped up and cried out awkwardly, "Hi Denise! Beautiful day, isn't it?"

"Yes, it is," she replied, but she wasn't smiling. Obviously she'd seen us sitting very close together. Her lips were pursed tightly shut as he looked from Anton to me.

"You know, Rachel," Anton said, motioning towards me as I got up too.

"Yes," she replied without smiling or looking at me, "of course I do. We met the first time when she visited with Albert two years ago. And now she's been helping in the kitchen quite a lot."

An awkward silence followed.

Then she did look at me and said, "Rachel, isn't it time we get back to the kitchen and start working on those squash we're going use for the soup tonight?"

Two days later, Denise asked me to go down to the storage cellar under the provision house and fetch a couple of big bottles of shoyu so we could refill the small bottles on the dinner tables in the dining hall. It was late afternoon and I was helping her in the kitchen with a few of the other people who were attending the retreat.

"Rachel," she said, pointing to the provisions house on the other side of the wide green lawn at the back of the monastery, "here are the keys to building. The cellar door is on the right, just after you walk into the house. The light switch is at the top of the stairs and you'll find the shoyu down there in the third room on the right. It's on one of the shelves. Bring up two of the big bottles, will you?"

"Sure," I said and headed out with the key. It was a bright, lovely afternoon and the woodlands surrounding the monastery were a symphony of color. I reveled in the fresh air and the beauty of the place. I took a deep breath and walked over to the provisions house.

I noticed I was actually feeling a little calmer, a little less distraught. It was as if my soul was beginning to settle down in this oasis of calm. I'd even started attending the meditations sessions again and was sometimes able to sit for fifteen or twenty minutes at a time and focus on my breathing. Just breathing, just one breath at a time. Breath in, breath out. Only that. Being mindful of the breath. Then my mind would go crazy again, running off on tangents, but I found I could come back to my breath again, just as Albert had taught me from the very beginning. Just let the thoughts be. Just allow them to arise and disappear again. Sometimes I even experienced short bursts of feeling calm and settled, of resting in that state of awareness. But then my monkey mind would take over again and it would pass.

I opened the door to the provisions house. I'd never been in there before and the house seemed deserted.

I found the door to the cellar and went down looking for the third room on the right. I found it and went in, and saw the shoyu bottles. I took two big bottles and left the room only to find myself face to face with Anton who was on his way down the hall.

We were both surprised to meet each other like that, all of a sudden without warning, and neither of us moved. I just stood there, staring into his deep, solemn eyes and he stared back at me, frozen to the spot.

Then he did something which surprised me – he leaned forward and kissed me on the mouth. And I did something which surprised me too – I let him! I let him kiss me, long and passionately and since I didn't move away, he put his arms around me and enveloped me in a warm, delicious embrace.

But then, just as suddenly, he let go of me and sprang back, crying, "Oh no, Rachel, what have I done? Please forgive me!" And with that he turned and bolted up the stairs and out of the house.

I just stood there, stunned. Staring at the empty space Anton left behind – and contemplating the warmth of his kiss and embrace. But then I remembered how he'd cried, "What have I done?"

But what in fact had he done?

I thought about it for a moment and all I could come up with was that he'd kissed me. What was wrong with that? Was it wrong because he thought he shouldn't be attracted to me? Was it wrong because he was a former sex addict in recovery? Was it wrong because he was my therapist? Was it wrong because he was Albert's friend? Was it wrong because I was wounded and vulnerable? Was it wrong because...

It didn't bear thinking about because it was what it was – just a kiss. And it was a lovely kiss at that. A passionate kiss... but still it was just a kiss!

I headed back to the kitchen.

The next day when I went for my session with Anton, I found him pacing up and down in his office as I entered the room.

He didn't look at me. When I closed the door behind me and walked over to his roomy couch, the one I always sat on during our sessions, he said very formally, "I must apologize for my behavior yesterday, Rachel." He was still standing.

When I didn't say anything, he continued, "It was totally unprofessional of me and I'm very sorry."

He just stood there, stiff as a board.

"Anton," I replied as I sat down, "you didn't do anything wrong."

"Oh yes, I did," he said. "You're my client and I'm your therapist," he continued and began pacing back and forth again. "It's just... unacceptable."

"Anton," I cried, "will you please stop and sit down and talk to me? Will you?"

But he kept on pacing back and forth.

"Anton, please."

He stopped and looked at me.

And as he did, it was as if all the air was sucked out of him.

He sat down next to me on the couch and put his head in his hands.

There was a long silence and I knew he was struggling with his inner demons.

Without looking up, he said, "You just don't understand, Rachel, I'm a Buddhist practitioner and the head of this monastery. And well... I've been celibate for almost five years now and it hasn't been a problem, even though there have been so many women passing through here... so many. But meeting you, I don't know what's happened to me. It's as if you've triggered something in me which I'd thought I'd conquered long ago."

There was a long silence.

My heart went out to him and I moved closer to him on the couch. I put my hand on his back, wanting to comfort him.

He didn't move away.

"There's just something about you," he muttered softly, more to himself than to me. "And the stories you've told me... I hate to admit it but they did more than disgust me... they aroused me too... The things Victor did to you, I want to do them to you, too. I want to..."

I pulled my hand away in surprise.

"Did you ever tie a woman up and hurt her?"

"No, never!" he cried, turning to face me with a look of anguish on his face. "I didn't mean it like that. But I did like bondage, but only if it was consensual."

"Oh, I see," I said softly. Suddenly I had this shaky, liquid feeling inside... thinking of Anton tying me up and...

"But when you told me about Victor tying you up – well I have to admit, it really aroused me." His voice was husky when he spoke.

I felt his hunger all the way down to my pussy.

Then he put his head back in his hands and groaned, "It's just more than I can handle, Rachel. It's just... oh God...what have I done?"

"But Anton..." I started to say but he didn't let me continue, instead he turned and looked at me again and said, "I know it's hard to understand but I've struggled with my addictions for so many years. It wasn't just the sex; I did drugs too for a while. I was such a mess when I was younger. Really! I was just so fucked up. And then finally, I ended up trying to kill myself. I really hit rock bottom. It was awful, a real nightmare, but eventually I got clean and went to meetings and to therapy. It was a long, hard road, but after some years, I pulled through and started a new life. I became a psychotherapist, began a relationship with Charlotte, and became a Buddhist practitioner. Things went really well for a long, long time. Charlotte and I moved up here and lived together. Five years ago, right after Charlotte and I broke up, I became head of the monastery. And after that, well, I've just dedicated my life to my work here and the path. But now, it's as if you've awakened something in me that I thought I'd never feel again... and I don't know what to do."

He was quiet for a while and then he moved away from me on the couch and got up.

"I don't think I can manage our session today, Rachel, so I think you'd better go," he said with real despair in his voice. "Let's just take a break for a couple of days, okay?"

I really felt for him; the anguish was written all over his face.

That night as I was lying in my bed in the bare room at the monastery... I got to thinking about her again... about good pussy bad pussy... I got to thinking...

What was she all about? Where had she led me and where was she leading me now?

And what about all the trouble she'd gotten me into before? And what about the innocence of her – the not knowing, the not knowing her power, the not knowing her seductiveness...

What was she all about?

And what now?

Where was she leading me?

What was going on?

Why the passion, the longing, the yearning? Why? Why?

I knew I was beautiful, sensual, and voluptuous...I knew she was beautiful, sensual, voluptuous...

I knew.

I knew she was impossible to resist... I knew I was impossible to resist...

I knew and even liked it. The energy of it, the power of good pussy bad pussy... the wild innocence of her... the magic of her...

What was this power she had, I had?

Where did it come from?

What did it mean?

Why? Why?

Where was she going?

Why was I the center of this force field?

Why did men love her so, love me so?

Why did they crave her, crave me, desire her, desire me, lust after her, lust after me so...?

Why? Why? Why?

Later that night, I was awakened by the sound of someone knocking softly on my door. I looked at the clock next to my bed. It was two in the morning. I got out of bed and tiptoed over to the door and said, "Who is it?" even though I knew who it was.

"Anton," said the husky voice on the other side of the door.

At first I wasn't sure what to do, though I wasn't surprised. Then I took a deep breath and opened the door. He rushed in and closed the door firmly behind him. Then he took me in his arms and began kissing me passionately.

"Oh, Rachel," he said as he smothered me with kisses; he was a man on fire.

His passion made me tremble as he slowly kissed my neck and then found his way to my shoulder. When he got there, he gently pushed my big nightshirt back from my shoulder.

I just stood there and let him, wondering, waiting to see if he would continue or turn and run again.

But this time, he didn't run and I felt the white hot heat he radiated.

He was burning with desire, burning with desire for me, and it was all coming out in one heady rush. And I had to admit, it was lovely, lovely to feel the heat he radiated, lovely to feel the passion that was consuming him. Hmmm… It, he, lit my fire. Hmmm… Because I was dry and shutdown like him, dry and yearning like him. In fact, we were both like a dry, scorched landscape that was yearning, yearning for rain, dry and yearning for warmth and love… I felt myself softening in his arms, almost swooning in the rush of it.

My breath quickened and I felt the heat rising in me too.

Then I felt my little pussy suddenly coming alive! There she was; the inner pulsing of her! Suddenly she was awake and alive and dancing her lusty little dance!

He was maneuvering me towards the bed and soon we were sitting on it and he was hungrily kissing my mouth again.

Then he stopped and took my face in his hands, "Oh, I know I shouldn't be doing this. I know it, Rachel, I know it, but I just can't help myself." He was a man possessed.

He sighed again and began kissing me, this time very slowly and very softly – and it felt ever so good and tender. As if my lips were soft, sweet-tasting buds that were opening at his touch as his tongue reached into me. Then, with a quick intake of breath, I felt how his hands found my breasts and how he began to caress them, finding my nipples, caressing them, pinching them gently as he continued to hungrily kiss my mouth.

I felt the wetness between my legs and lay back on the bed almost swooning. He moved with me.

"Rachel, you're so beautiful," he was murmuring. "May I see you? May I..."

The feeling was so intense that I couldn't answer him. But he understood that now I wanted him too, and he began pulling my nightshirt up over my head.

We were both breathing heavily now... murmuring... sighing... swaying together... moving together... he was unbuttoning his shirt and I was helping him with his pants buckle, and then his pants, and...

My pussy was wet, wet and getting wetter. She was wanting him now, right now and not wanting to wait... oh no, oh no, no more waiting, just fill me, touch me, take me now...

Then we were both naked and melting into each other in one heady embrace and he mounted me and entered me fiercely as if there was no time. His need was that great, and so was mine. Oh, yes! We were both in a hurry and both wanted it now. Now! And fast. It had to happen fast and now. Please now! Because both of us had gone hungry for so long, both of us had been yearning for so long, there was no time for leisurely foreplay. No time for... it just had to be...Now... It had to be orgasm and ecstatic release, now. That was what we both wanted, needed, craved, desired... oh so badly, ever so badly...and I felt myself melting, merging into him as he held me tightly to him, breathing hard and then boom, there it was! We both exploded at the very same moment, pounding into each other as the stars and the sky exploded in us and around us.

Afterwards I found myself in his arms, weeping.

He held me tightly to him as I wept.

But I was inconsolable. Weeping and weeping.

"What is it, Rachel?" he asked softly.

But I couldn't stop crying; it was as if another tidal wave of despair was sweeping over me - again. I felt that terrible emptiness, again – that incredible longing for Albert, again – like a sharp pain in my gut. All I could do was sob into Anton's chest, "But I love him so... I do, I do, I do... I just can't do this! I just can't..." And the bitterness of it all was like the darkness of night closing in on me again. Just as it had done that night when I had run hysterically out of the meditation hall and collapsed on the cold ground. It was happening again; the darkness was closing in around me.

"Oh, poor babe," he said soothingly, "it's okay! I know you love him, I know you do. It's okay..."

When I heard his words, I cried, "And I don't even know if he's alive or dead!" And then I convulsed into another spasm of weeping.

Anton just lay there perfectly still and held me as I wept.

When I woke up in the morning, Anton was already gone. Apparently I'd slept through the morning bell because I heard the sound of people in the hallway; it sounded like they were coming back from breakfast and on their way to morning meditation.

That day at our session, Anton began by asking me how I felt after being with him the night before. He didn't approach me physically or try to hold me or anything, we were sitting in our usual client-therapist seating. Me on the couch, him in his armchair.

I thought about his question for a while because I wanted to be completely honest with him when I answered. "Well, you know I'm attracted to you and wanted you as much as you wanted me. But as you saw, our lovemaking also awakened that terrible feeling of loss I've got inside about Albert."

When he heard my words, Anton got up and started pacing the room. "I know, I know. Oh God, Rachel, I know. I should have just left you alone! It was so unprofessional of me to come to your room like that in the middle of the night. I don't know what's happening to me. It's like I can't control myself anymore."

When I didn't reply, he stopped abruptly in the middle of the room and said, "I hope to God no one's knows that I've been with you."

"I doubt if anyone knows you came to my room last night," I said slowly. "But I think Denise might suspect something's going on between us. After all, she did see us sitting close together under the oak tree the other day."

"Oh my God, no, Rachel! Do you realize what that would mean? It would be such a scandal if people found out. No one would ever forgive me. Me, the head of the monastery, sleeping with a woman who was here on retreat and who is under my care! Can't you just see it?"

Now it was my turn to comfort him.

"Oh, come on, Anton, no one is going to find out. We always keep a proper distance from each other when we're in the meditation hall or dining hall. Why would anyone suspect anything?"

"But what about Denise? She notices everything," he cried. "I'm sure she knows!"

The day after, when I was coming out of the afternoon meditation session, Anton was waiting for me. There were people around, so we couldn't really talk but he said he just wanted to see how I was doing. I guess he figured a question like that would seem okay if anyone overheard us because everyone at the retreat knew about Albert's abduction and how devastated I was.

When I said I was going for a little walk, he followed me out of the monastery. When we were out of earshot of other people, he asked me to come to his house later that evening, after dinner, when no one would notice.

"Just for a little talk," he said.

I stopped for a moment and considered his request. I wasn't sure how I felt after what had happened between us.

"Just to talk," he said again softly, almost pleading.

The way he said that really got me so I figured it would be okay to visit him.

"Okay, Anton, I'll come around eight," I said, thinking why not? What could happen that hadn't already happened anyway. "I guess you're right, talking can't hurt."

He smiled when I said yes and seemed his usual calm self again. Which I had to admit, I really liked. I found him very attractive when he wasn't so freaked out.

His house was halfway down the forest road that led from the monastery to the rehab center where he also worked as a psychotherapist. He'd already told me about his job there and how he tried to help the addicts in rehab understand their addictions and stay clean. According to him, it wasn't an easy job. But I thought if anyone was qualified for a job like that, it must be him – because he had quite a past. Which I had to admit made him very attractive too. I liked the fact that he was hip to the ways of the world and wasn't just a Buddhist practitioner who had no experience of everyday life and the so-called "real world". So yes, there was just something about him I was really drawn to.

As I was walking towards his house that evening, I found myself wondering how I might have felt about Anton if I wasn't still so madly in love with Albert.

But what about Albert?

Was he even alive?

I had this terrible sinking feeling inside every time I thought about him.

It was the beginning of November now and almost a year since Albert had been abducted in mid-December last year. And five months had passed since Jacques Durand from the French Foreign Ministry had called and told me they'd lost all contact with Albert's abductors, and that I should prepare myself for the worst. Five months!

I felt sick every time I thought of it.

Since June, there hadn't been a word – not a single word nor the slightest sign or murmur from anyone, anywhere in the Middle East to indicate anything about Albert's whereabouts or whether he was even alive. Nothing. Nothing whatsoever! So what was I to think? Or do? Should I go on hoping against hope, believing no matter what? Or should I face what could be the reality of Albert never coming back... of Albert not being alive anymore... oh it didn't bear thinking about. It just didn't.

So there I was, on my way to Anton's house, not knowing if the man I loved was even alive and not knowing how I should feel about this new man in my life. An interesting, exciting man who had just made passionate love to me two nights ago. All I did know was that I was feeling slightly tingly all over – and shaky and unsure of myself because I had no idea what was going to happen next. On the one hand, I felt really drawn to Anton and the way he could swing between being serious and spiritual, to being passionate and all fucked up. That really turned me on. But then, something about making love to him the other night had again triggered the awful pain of losing Albert, the awful pain of not knowing whether Albert was dead or alive, that terrible uncertainty, the anguish, the grief. It all welled up in me again after I made love to Anton. And the fact that the lovemaking with Anton was so good, made it all seem that much worse!

Anton's house appeared around the bend in the forest road. In fact, it wasn't a house at all but a log cabin. It looked very quaint and idyllic there in the middle of the forest, with smoke coming out of the chimney. It was early November and the evening air was chill, with a hint of winter in it so it was nice to think there would be a warm, crackling fire in the fireplace.

My heart thumped as I approached his front door. I'd never been in his house before. Would he want to make love to me again even if he said he just wanted to talk? But of course he would. Of course! No sense pretending I didn't know. No, the big question was how would I react? How would it feel to be alone with him again – in his house? All I knew for sure was that I had that liquidy feeling down there as I knocked on his door.

About half an hour later, we were sitting on his couch in front of the crackling fire and Anton was explaining to me, "According to Buddhist philosophy, there are three moments when it is particularly easy to attain, or at least get a glimpse of, the enlightened mind – and that is when we sneeze, have an orgasm, and at the moment of death."

"Really!" I exclaimed, surprised that orgasm could have anything to do with enlightenment. "When we have orgasm?"

"Yes," he replied, "or at least that's what the Buddhists say. They say it is because when we have an orgasm, we experience the complete release of all thought processes, at least for a moment. And this gives us a chance to experience what they call the Clear Light of Rigpa, which is our original nature.

"Rigpa?"

"Yes, and by that they mean the field of pure consciousness, which is our true nature... The highly trained practitioner is able to consciously experience this when he or she goes beyond the thought processes, beyond thought or thinking... "

He paused and the fire crackled and leaped before us.

"And the connection to orgasm?" I asked.

"Well, just think about what happens when you have a really good orgasm..." he replied softly. "It's like everything is gone – just blown away... forgotten... and all you feel is this incredible bliss. There is nothing else... the whole world has disappeared... everything... every thought, every worry, every care is completely gone... at least for a moment or two... or maybe even three... if you're lucky."

He was so right.

Everything disappears when you have a good orgasm...

I sighed and giggled softly at his words... and when I did, he said gently, "Rachel, will you let me tie you up and make love to you?"

His words really caught me by surprise, considering what we were just talking about.

"What?" I gasped, feeling chills run up and down my spine.

"Will you let me tie you up and make love to you?"

His voice was husky in that special way and even though he wasn't looking at me, I felt the intensity of his desire.

Tie me up and make love to me?

I felt my whole system reacting with shock.

I remembered back to the time when Victor tied me up and so brutally forced me to surrender to his will. It had been so confusing and degrading. Now Anton – *my new lover and therapist* – was asking for the same thing. How could it be?

When I didn't reply, he turned and put his arm around me and pulled me to him. I didn't resist. I could feel the heat radiating from him. He lifted my face towards his and began kissing my mouth. I felt his hunger and how it reached all the way down to my pussy. Before he began telling me about Buddhist philosophy and orgasm, we had been talking about what had happened between him and me so far. And I tried to explain to him why I felt so devastated after we made love for the first time, the other night.

And he let me.

He was easy to talk to when he was calm like that.

He didn't try to comfort me or anything – or interfere in anyway. He just let me be myself and own my own feelings.

I liked that, and the restful quietness I often experienced when I was with him.

But the restful calm was definitely broken when he asked me if he could tie me up and make love to me. I just couldn't get my head around it.

His hands had already found my breasts and I was sighing softly at his touch.

"May I," he said again, insisting that I answer. "I need to know because I need to see you like that, Rachel."

"But why?"

"Because I can't get the thought of Victor tying you up and tormenting you like he did out of my mind... which is why I want to do it too. But not to torment you. I want to give you another experience... a pleasurable one, an ecstatic one... one that is far, far better than what happened with him... if you'll let me, if you'll trust me. I promise you, you won't regret it."

I trembled at the intensity of his words. There was just something about the way he said it that made me shiver all over. It was like we were suddenly entering another realm, another energy field. I had the feeling that if I let him, he would take me to a place I'd never been to before – that was how intense he was.

"You know you can trust me. I would never do anything to hurt you."

I trembled at the thought of being wholly in his power, at his mercy.

He had unfastened my bra and was pinching my nipples with just enough pressure to make me want more... much, much more.

"Will you let me, Rachel? Will you?"

I was on the bed, spread eagle, all tied up and Anton was brushing my thighs ever so softly, ever so gently with a large feather, just as Victor had done. But this time, it was so different because Anton was so tender and loving as he moved the feather ever so gently, slowly up and down my thighs and then along my hips and stomach. And every time he came close to my pussy, the feeling was so intense that it sent me writhing in an ecstasy of wanting him. Of wanting him in me, deep in me.

"You are so beautiful, Rachel," he said ever so softly as he blew the feather gently along my belly towards my aching pussy.

I heard myself moaning and saw myself twisting and turning with desire, but because I was spread eagle and tied up, I couldn't throw myself at him even though I desperately wanted to. All I could do was moan and twist and turn and say, "Please Anton... oh, please!"

When he heard the desperation in my voice, he realized he was going too fast and it was getting too intense, so he gently pulled back and dropped the feather.

Then instead of teasing and tantalizing me further with the feather, he leaned towards me and kissed my mouth without touching my body at all. All he did was kiss my lips slowly and sensually, as if he had all the time in the world. Which only made me want him more and moan more. It was so intense. He was so intense! I shut my eyes and felt my body trying to press itself towards him – but I couldn't, I couldn't.

I moaned as my body tingled all over with longing and pleasure.

"Oh, Anton, please!" I heard myself begging, but all he did was move slowly down to my breasts and kiss them and then take each one of my nipples into his mouth, pinching each one, with just enough pressure to drive me mad with desire.

Yes, he was driving me mad.

All I wanted was for him to touch me and fuck me and release me.

But he didn't and wouldn't, not yet anyway. It was maddening. Maddening!

Instead he pulled back and leisurely took off his shirt. He had this wonderful, lean body and I wanted him to stop tormenting me and take me, possess me, and ravish me right away. I wanted him to fuck me so badly; my pussy was that wet, that ready. But he wasn't ready yet, so he didn't and wouldn't. At least not yet. Instead he leaned back towards me and took me by the hips and held them which drove me crazy with desire and then he leaned forward and put his mouth to my pussy, making me groan again. Oh God, it was good... oh God, he was good! Feeling his mouth on me in that way... I was only a hair's breath away from orgasm.

I was that close.

He knew I couldn't wait much longer.

So he released me and got up and regarded me from the foot of the bed.

Then he took off his pants. His manhood sprang forth and stood erect, pulsing and wanting me too. Seeing him like that I knew he couldn't wait much longer either, naked as he was, standing at the foot of the bed, admiring me as I admired him and longed for him to take me.

"Anton, please!" I moaned, my little pussy trembling with desire. "Please come to me!"

He was a beautiful man, strong and lean and angular with a shock of brownish, blond hair and deep, solemn eyes. He leaned forward and picked up the feather and began caressing my thighs again.

"My God, you are so beautiful, Rachel," he said as he moved slowly towards me, kissing my thighs and stomach, and then touching my wet pussy gently with his fingers. "Open up to me now, baby! Now!"

And I did, and I was, as I moaned and he mounted me.

I was trembling all over.

Trembling. Yearning. Wanting…

"Tell me… tell me… is it nice… do you want it?" he whispered in my ear as his throbbing penis touched my pussy. "Tell me… do you?"

"Oh, yes! Yes!" I cried, writhing, almost unable to contain myself, trying to press myself up towards his waiting cock. "Please Anton, please! I can't wait any longer!"

And with that, he literally slammed himself into me. Hard and fast. Deep and dark. It was a shock, it was paradise, it was bliss, it was incredible.

I had him inside me. Finally!

"Ooooohhh," I cried.

"Yes, baby! Yes!" he cried back as he pumped himself deep

into me.

I felt myself writhing around his penis as he moved deeper and deeper into me.

"Now, let me see you dance!" he cried.

And with that, I exploded all around him writhing and sighing as he pumped and pumped and finally exploded deep in the depths of me too.

The next day at our session, the contrast between Anton's wisdom and sexual prowess the night before, and his inner torment was even more apparent. In a way, it was hard to believe this was the same man. The same man who had given me the most amazing sexual experience just the night before. Because that was exactly what he'd done. He'd said he would pleasure me in a way I'd never been pleasured before – and he did. The tying me up, the way he touched me and tormented me ever so gently and lovingly with the feather had brought me to the most ecstatic experience I'd had in a very long time. It was truly amazing and oh so delicious. So he was right that the pleasure I experienced in his loving hands, did, at least somewhat, make up for the abuse I'd suffered at the hands of Victor.

But now, sitting across from him in his office, listening to him talk, it was a shock to find him once again so conflicted and so much at crosscurrents with himself.

"It's driving me crazy," he was saying softly. "You're driving me crazy... I just don't know what to do."

"But, Anton," I cried out in surprise, "it was you who wanted to make love. I thought we were just going to talk."

"Oh, I know, I know, and now I regret it and hate myself for doing it. It's just you're so fantastic, Rachel... so... I just can't keep my hands off you." He got up and started pacing back and forth across the room again. "Oh God, what if someone finds out about us? It would be such a scandal. I can't bear to think about it."

All I could think of watching him pace up and down the floor was well, ok yes, so he really wanted to fuck me and he did. Why was he making such a big deal out of doing something he really wanted to do? It just didn't make sense. Why was he torturing himself like that by regretting the pleasure we shared? It was as if he hated himself for being a man with strong sexual desires. It was both funny and sad to watch.

And I loved and hated him for being so conflicted. I guess because I understood him so well, understood the conflict so well. He was the male version of the good pussy bad pussy thing I experienced myself. Yes, that was it! He had the good cock bad cock thing! He wanted it and he didn't. And then he wanted it some more and then he didn't. It was driving him crazy. Because when his body took over, he simply couldn't control himself. That's how powerful the sex drive is – which is exactly what he told me during our therapy sessions. So the reality was, he was just as hooked on sex as I was, just as confused and tormented and enchanted by sex as I was! No wonder he was on the spiritual pathway, seeking and longing for enlightenment and liberation from the bondage of our desires.

My heart went out to him.

But at that moment, I also realized that although I was truly fond of the man, I wasn't in love with him.

"Poor Anton," I said and got up from the couch, suddenly understanding that he was incapable of figuring this out by himself. I had to help him.

So I walked over and stood in front of him. He stopped pacing back and forth and just stood there, looking at me, waiting for me to speak. I put my hands on his shoulders and looked into his kind, handsome, tormented face and said, "Our being together probably isn't such a good idea, Anton. Not for you and not for me. So why don't we just drop the whole thing for a while?"

When he heard my words, a look of relief washed over his beautiful, tormented face.

Then I kissed him softly on the cheek and tiptoed out of

his office.

The next day, I was feeling calmer so I joined the morning meditation session. When the session was over, the sun was shining brightly and it was a wonderful day, so I decided to go and sit under the old oak tree one more time. As I was sitting there, all alone, I realized I should go back to New York even if the three-week retreat wasn't over yet. I just knew I should. Knew it was the best thing to do, all things taken into consideration. So I took a deep breath and decided I'd go back to my room, pack my stuff, and go back to the city right away. I was so lost in thought I didn't notice Anton approaching. But there he was, sitting down next to me. He didn't say a word, but just sat.

I was the first to break the silence.

"Anton," I said, "I've decided to go back to New York."

He looked at me in surprise.

"What, now?"

"Yes, now," I said.

"But why?"

"Because I think it's best. It's the best thing for both of us."

He started to speak, but just at that moment, there was the sound of a helicopter flying overhead. We looked up. Sure enough, a helicopter was flying low over the forest, heading straight towards the monastery.

"Did you see that?" cried Anton, jumping up. "I wonder what's going on!"

I jumped up too and we both started heading back towards the monastery as fast as we could.

"No one ever comes here in a chopper," Anton cried as we rushed back to see what was going on.

And sure enough, it looked like the chopper was positioning itself right over the grounds behind the monastery, making ready to land. As we approached, we could see the ruckus had caused almost everyone else to come rushing out of the monastery too.

Then the chopper slowly started to land as we all stood there, watching. It was a small chopper and as it got closer to the ground, I could see there were only two men in it. One was the pilot and the other was a dark-haired man sitting next to him.

The machine got closer, hovering over the ground in the middle of the monastery lawn, and that was when I realized that my heart was pounding like crazy in my chest.

There was something about the dark-haired man sitting next to the pilot that seemed...

Oh my God!

Who is the dark-haired man sitting next to the pilot??????

Who is the dark-haired man?

Oh my God...

I felt myself trembling all over and began to run towards the machine as it was about to land.

The dark haired man!

Who could it be?

Who is it?

Oh my God!

Could it be?

But yes...

I can't believe my eyes!

But can I be sure... is it really...

Is it...??

Is it...??

It is...!

IT IS!!!

IT'S...

ALBERT!!!

ALBERT!!!

Now I was running as fast as I could. Running for dear life! As soon as the chopper landed, the door sprang open and Albert jumped out and was running towards me too.

It all seemed to be happening in slow motion because it felt as if I couldn't get to him fast enough.

ALBERT!!!

ALBERT!!!

I was crying his name, crying *ALBERT* and then it happened; we collided in a frenzy of hugging and kissing, toppling onto the ground in ecstatic joy!

And I was touching his face, kissing his lips and he was touching my face and kissing my lips back.

"I can't believe it's you – oh my darling! I can't believe it! You're alive," and I was kissing him and hugging him and touching him.

That was when I realized that I was laughing and crying at the same time.

"Yes, it's me, my darling! I'm alive!"

"But I can't believe it!"

It was as if I was in a dream and was afraid I was going to wake up.

"I was so afraid you were dead!"

Now we were sitting on the lawn and he was holding me and I was laughing and crying.

"So afraid!"

"Yes, I know," he said softly, stroking my hair.

"But you're not."

"No I'm not."

"And you're here now and you're alive," I cried again as if I wasn't quite sure it was true. "You're alive!"

"Yes, my darling. I am," he said and laughed out loud again.

"Oh my God, oh my God! I'm so grateful. So grateful!" I exclaimed, and with that more tears came and I looked up and realized Anton was motioning everyone to go back into the monastery to give us some space.

That was when I found myself touching Albert all over. Just to make sure he wasn't a dream. Just to make sure it was really him. And he was smoothing down my hair and looking at me so lovingly.

"But you're so skinny!" I cried as I felt his arms and chest through his leather jacket.

"Yes I know. Can't say there was much to eat for a very long time."

"Oh, my darling!" I cried again, throwing my arms around him, hugging him to me with all my might. Not ready to think about what he must have been through.

"Oh, my love, I'm so glad you're alive," I cried again, "I love you so much!"

And with that, we hugged and kissed each other hungrily and hugged and kissed some more.

And... time just seemed to stand still...

And...

Then... a little while later, Anton came out of the monastery holding a key chain. We were still sitting on the ground, hugging and holding each other, but when we saw Anton approaching, we got up.

Albert and Anton embraced.

"God, it's good to see you," said Anton warmly.

"God, it's good to be here," replied Albert, just as warmly.

Anton stuck out his hand, "Here's the key to the guesthouse. Now you two get over there before you both freeze to death, sitting here on the cold ground."

"Thanks," said Albert, taking the key. "Talk to you later."

Then as we turned to go, he pointed to the chopper and said to me, "Oh, I almost forgot, I need to have a word with my pilot, Jason."

After he sent Jason away, we walked slowly, hand in hand, to the guesthouse. Slowly, savoring every step. Savoring...

And I felt my heart singing!

Albert!

Albert is back!

Albert is alive!

ALBERT IS ALIVE!

ALIVE!

Once inside, we took off our jackets and turned on the heat full blast. Then Albert swept me off my feet and promptly carried me upstairs to the bedroom. We both knew the house because we'd stayed there when we visited the monastery together almost two years ago. And even then, Albert knew the house well, having stayed there many times before.

He put me down on the big bed, and immediately we were hugging and kissing and holding on to each other with an urgency that was almost painful. We'd both thought we'd lost each other forever so now we weren't completely sure we'd really found each other again. Maybe this was only a dream, only a short reprieve from the nightmare of loss we'd suffered, and we'd wake up again to that terrible ache of loss.

So we cling desperately to each other. Desperately!

The hunger was palpable, intense, real.

Albert was the first to understand what was happening.

"Come, my darling," he whispered softly in my ear, "maybe we should get undressed."

When he said that, I laughed out loud, and with my laughter, some of the tension seemed to evaporate. We both sat up and struggled out of our clothes and then when they were off, we snuggled under the covers. But there it was again, the fear of losing each other again and the intensity of our need. So we clung desperately to each other, smothering each other with kisses and then he was touching my body, my breasts, sighing this great, wonderful sigh and I was wet, wet, wet, wanting him so desperately , wanting him, oh, wanting him. And there he was, inside me because he couldn't wait, and inside me because I couldn't wait. And it was oh so good, oh so very good, and he was holding me to him in a way no man had ever held me, with such ferocious dedication and appreciation and passion and love. It was so powerful and divine that we were both swept away by the power of our devotion to each other. And then, in one fast, intense, powerful rush, we exploded together at the exact same moment like a thousand million stars, crying aloud to the heavens for the pure unadulterated joy of it.

Later, when I was all snuggled up in his arms, I realized that Albert was sound asleep. It was late afternoon and only a couple of hours since he returned. We'd been in bed for a while, both basking in the afterglow of our glorious reunion and lovemaking when I realized that Albert was sleeping. I lay very still and tried not to move or wake him because I was starting to realize how exhausted he must be from his ordeal. Maybe now was the first time he'd been able to relax in God knows how long.

Suddenly he cried out and sat up in the bed, looking disoriented.

"It's okay, Albert, darling," I cried, sitting up too.

He was looking around the room as if he didn't know where he was.

"Everything is ok, darling." I said softly, taking his face in my hands. "Everything is ok. You're with me and you're safe, my darling.

The light came back in his eyes and he grabbed me to him, holding me tight.

"It's okay, baby," I whispered softly as we rocked back and forth, "it's okay…"

"I thought I was back…" his words faded into the silence.

"Oh, darling! You're here with me now and we're in New York, at the monastery."

"I know, I know…" There were tears on his cheeks.

We sat like that for a long while in the fading light of the afternoon.

When he'd calmed down once again, we both lay back in the bed again, and he dozed off.

A little later, after we'd snuggled again for a while, I asked him how long he'd been out of captivity.

"It's only been seven or eight days since I got out of Yemen. A little more than a week."

"Oh, my God, you really were in Yemen?"

"Yes."

"What were you doing there? Can you tell me just a little – or is it too painful to talk about?"

He was silent for a while and then he said slowly, "I don't know why my captors took me to Yemen... but by the time we got there, I was so sick and delirious and weak from all the ketamine they were giving me to knock me out every time they moved me... and that... combined with the lack of food and water, well, I was just about dead anyway."

I held him tightly as he spoke. As far as I knew, ketamine was a sedative they gave to animals.

"I am so lucky to be alive. If it wasn't for Safa and her friends, I would be dead now."

"Who's Safa?"

"She's the little Yemeni woman who saved my life."

"Safa..." I said softly, letting her name roll slowly over my lips. "I love her already."

"Yes, I knew you would, and so do I."

"What did she do? How did she save you?"

When he didn't answer, I said, "Can you tell me? Or is it too difficult to talk about it?"

He cleared his throat and continued slowly, "Well, I can try." And then he fell silent, as if thinking back. Finally he said, "Well, it was about seven or eight weeks ago and we'd arrived in Sanaa, the capital of Yemen, though I didn't know it at the time. I was tied up as usual in another crummy, boiling, hot room, sick and delirious and pretty much contemplating my approaching death when I became aware that a fierce gun battle was raging all around me. My captors were fighting with...well I really don't know who they were fighting with. Apparently there are so many different armed militant groups in that country at the moment and they're all vying for power and control. One group more radical than the other..."

He paused again for a while as if it was almost too painful to speak about it.

I didn't press him but just cradled him in my arms instead.

He was trembling slightly and my heart ached as I began to contemplate some of the horrors he went through during his captivity.

After a while he continued, "But as I said, I was all tied up and so weak and delirious, there wasn't much I could do. And eventually I must have passed out. How long I was out, I have no idea... but suddenly I was awakened in the middle of the night by two figures completely covered in black Niqabs."

"Niqabs" I asked, "What's that?"

"They are those full-face, black burkas the women wear which completely cover them from head to toe, with only a slit for the eyes. Anyway, I was so disoriented I didn't really know what was going on. The one – the little one – spoke a little English and hurriedly told me we had to get out of there if I wanted to live. So they cut me loose and literally lifted me up and dragged me out of that room. Looking back I don't know how those two women managed to get me out of there and all the way down the alley to their place. Fortunately, it wasn't that far away. But the bravery of it! The strength and courage it demanded. You have no idea..."

"So the little one was Safa?"

"Yes," he replied slowly, all choked up. "She and her friend Alaa risked their lives to save me. If we had been caught, they would be dead now too."

"Oh, my God," was all I could say, trying to imagine little Safa and her friend dragging Albert down that alleyway in the middle of the night.

"They took me to the women's quarters behind one of the

houses further down the street. And there I passed out again. So it was touch and go for many days as Safa and her friends nursed me back to life. It turned out she is one of the few women in Yemen who is studying to be a doctor and she was interning at the local hospital. Which was fortunate for me because that meant she had access to drugs and medical advice."

That was when I noticed we were both crying, thinking about this little Yemeni woman who had saved my beloved's life.

"How can we ever thank her and her friends?" I exclaimed.

"We will find a way, I am sure, my darling, we will find a way," Albert said, first drying my tears and then his own. "I promise you – I am determined to find a way to help them. I will never forget what she and her friends did for me. You have no idea what it's like there for women... no idea."

"But how did you get from there, from that place of hiding, to freedom?"

"It wasn't easy. I was there in hiding in their women's quarters for about six or seven weeks. It was only first after about ten days that the fever broke and I was no longer delirious. After that, it took all those weeks to nurse me back to this. At first, I was so weak I couldn't even sit up or get up. But slowly, slowly, Safa and her friends fed me this thin gruel and slowly, slowly I began to regain my strength."

"As I got stronger, I too started wondering how I would ever escape from my hideout because they told me – or at least Safa told me – she was the only one who spoke a little English – that the militants who captured me were combing the area, trying to find me. So we were all pretty scared that they would find me again. Once, they even came to the women's quarters but the women put me in a black Niqab and raised such a ruckus screaming and shouting at the men telling them they couldn't come in that they eventually gave up and left. You have no idea how much noise those women can make if they want to. I was amazed."

I smiled at the thought of Safa and her friends defending Albert, all covered up in a black Niqab.

"What bravery! So what happened then?"

"Well, Safa had a friend at the local hospital whose brother worked as an interpreter at the French embassy. Finally, and I don't really know how, they convinced him he had to help get me through the streets of Sanaa to the French embassy. And he did."

"But how?"

"Well, they cooked up this elaborate plan, decking me out as a woman again in a black Niqab and driving me and several other women in the back of the van with Malik, the interpreter, and his friend Ahmed at the wheel. The story was – if we got stopped – that we were on our way to a marketplace on the other side of town to go shopping for a friend's wedding. Our route just accidentally passed the French embassy compound at a pre-determined time when the embassy guards knew we would be coming. You see, Safa and her friends finally convinced Malik that he had to tell the embassy staff what was going on.

"So anyway… when we got there, I jumped out at the pre-arranged time… just when the gate was opening and ran – as fast as I could – into the compound, right before the gate slammed shut behind me. Malik and his friends sped off before I could look even back. It was vitally important that if it was discovered it was me, that I could in no way be connected to them.

"Once I was inside, the French embassy staff took care of me and then we had to figure out a way to get me out of Yemen alive. Which wasn't that easy either because there are no direct flights out of Yemen, and because the militants were still hunting for me all over Sanaa. Five million Euros is a lot of ransom money."

"So you knew how much they were asking for you?"

"Yes, I knew that from the beginning, before I got so desperately ill."

That was when I realized Albert was really trembling.

"Are you okay, darling?" I asked, kissing him gently.

"Yeah," he said slowly. "It's just sometimes I get the shakes when I think about all the things that happened. I've been experiencing this quite often the last few days." But then he stopped and took a few deep breaths. We were both quiet for a while.

When the trembling subsided a bit, Albert said, "Rachel, will you go over to the monastery and get us some food. I'm absolutely famished."

"But of course," I cried and jumped up. "Why didn't I think of feeding you sooner?"

We both laughed.

"And get your iPhone too so I can see the pictures of Isabella. I can't believe I haven't seen our daughter in almost a year."

I pulled on my jeans and sweater and was putting on my boots when Albert said, "Don't be gone too long, darling. I don't think I can bear it."

The look of anguish on his face told me he wasn't kidding.

After that, we spent the rest of the day in bed, eating, looking at pictures of Isabella, making love, and sometimes crying.

Albert was a mess and I was too.

We were all over the place emotionally – one minute up and the next minute down – and our lovemaking was ravenous. It was as if we were both afraid we might be torn from each other the very next minute. We kissed and hugged and made love, over and over again until we were utterly exhausted.

"You know the embassy doctor said it would take a while to get over something like this," Albert said as we were dozing off once again in each other's arms. "It's not going to be easy."

"Shhh, darling…" I replied softly. "It's going to be okay. I'm sure we'll make it through."

"He said I would probably need professional help to deal with the trauma of it."

"If that's what it takes, then we'll do it," I repeated again softly. "We'll do whatever it takes… Oh darling, just remember how much I love you! I love you, I love you."

I covered him with kisses and with that, we fell asleep.

He woke up several times during the night in a sweat, trembling and looking around the room in panic. But as soon as he realized that I was there with him and that we were in the guest house at the monastery, he calmed down and fell back asleep. I held him tightly the whole night through.

In the morning, he seemed a little better, a little calmer. But he wouldn't let me out of his sight; it was as if he couldn't bear it. I felt the same way; so we clung to each other, all day long and all night long.

Once in a while, another tiny bit or piece of information about his terrible ordeal would come out, but I didn't press him. Somehow I knew not to. But the more I heard of his story, the more I understood how incredible it was that he was alive.

Oh, Albert! Albert!

Two days later, we were both a little calmer, but only a little. Albert was desperate to see Isabella so we decided to head back to New York – to my mother's house where the children were staying with my mother and Amélie. Albert seemed genuinely happy when he heard that Amélie had come to New York with me and the children.

As we approached my mother's house on Long Island, I felt I had to remind him that little Isabella probably would not recognize him. "Just remember, darling, she was only eight months old the last time she saw you. Now she's almost a year and eight months old and becoming quite the little lady. I just want you to remember it's not a sign that she doesn't love you if she doesn't recognize you immediately. Just give her a little time to get to know you again."

But the funny thing was, she did remember him!

When we walked into the living room, Albert just sat down on the floor and wept when he saw her standing there, looking at him with her big brown eyes. And then little Isabella came toddling over to him and threw her arms around him – to comfort him! It was a miracle! We all laughed and cried together. Albert, my mother, Amélie, Daniel and I. Tears of joy!

I got another surprise at dinner that evening. When my mother said something about us going back to the loft in Soho, Albert turned to her and said, "Isabel, would you mind if we stayed here for a while? I just don't think my nervous system can handle the big city yet – and it's so nice and quiet here."

"But, of course," she exclaimed immediately. "I love would to have you all!"

"I hope it's not too much of an imposition, but as you can see, I'm feeling pretty shaky at the moment. And I can see the children are so happy here. It would do my heart good if we could stay here for a while."

"But of course!" she cried, giving him her warmest and most loving smile from across the table where she was sitting. "Dearest Albert, you can stay here as long as you want. We all love you so much and are so incredibly grateful to have you back alive. Nothing would make me happier than to have you here in my house."

So it was settled. And it seemed to take a weight off his shoulders. As if it gave him a little more time to regain his balance and get acclimatized to the world again before he went public. He'd already told me that the French government had agreed to keep his miraculous escape secret until he was ready to release the news.

Thus the days passed. And there was something about him spending time with little Isabella that seemed to heal him right before our eyes. He could sit on the floor and play with her for hours, or toddle around with her on the grounds around my mother's house. It was a joy to behold.

My mother also helped Albert get in touch with one of the leading trauma therapists in the New York area, doctor and psychotherapist Leonard Jacobs. Since Albert was still in hiding,

Jacobs agreed to come to the house almost every other day to work with Albert and to help him come to terms with the terrible trauma he'd experienced.

Sometimes the doctor would invite me to join one of their sessions so I could better understand what Albert was going through and support him in his recovery. Sometimes Jacobs would also have a session with me and my mother alone to help us understand the dynamics of trauma and trauma healing.

Some days were tougher than others, but little by little, Albert seemed to be getting better. He had fewer nightmares and his nervous system seemed to be calming down. Occasionally – at the most unexpected moments – another bit or piece of his ordeal would come out; even though I never pressed him to talk about it. It would just happen. Something would trigger the memory in him and he'd suddenly stop and say something like, "Rachel, darling, do you see the way that ray of light is shining through the window?" And when I'd look, he'd explain, "It reminds me of how it was... of how... well sometimes, on a good day during my captivity... I could get lost watching the light dancing as it penetrated through to me in whatever miserable hellhole they were hiding me in..." When I'd look at him, there were often tears in his eyes and that terrible look of anguish would appear on his face again. But then, he would breathe deeply as Doctor Jacobs recommended and try to allow and accept whatever he was feeling and whatever his body was doing. Then slowly, slowly the moment of anguish would pass.

But more than anything, the simple pleasure of being with me and Isabella again brought him joy and healing – and often tears of gratitude. The morning little Isabella looked up at him and said, "Papa!" for the first time, he wept openly.

A week or two later, I got a little more insight into the anguish Albert was feeling. It was late at night and I was standing in the middle of the bedroom, completely naked. Albert was holding my hips and looking at me. He'd asked me to get undressed so he could see me naked. So of course I did. I loved it when it seemed like the old Albert was back, when he seemed to be more himself again and could revel in me and the joy of our being together. I found it profoundly pleasurable to be able to please him as I did.

He was down on his knees, holding my hips and gazing up at me with such love and adoration in his eyes. It was intoxicating indeed, and I was overwhelmed with gratitude that Life, the Universe or whatever you want to call it, had brought his wonderful, amazing man back to me again.

Oh, Albert!

I love you so much!

I'm so grateful to have you back alive!

"Darling," he was saying, looking up at me with eyes of love, "I want to make you pregnant again."

"What?" I laughed in surprise. Sometimes he said the most amazing things.

"No, seriously," he said, "I want to make you pregnant again. I can't explain it, but just the thought of making you pregnant again is making me dizzy with desire!"

He was standing up now, taking me in his arms, smoothing down my wild hair, and then lifting me up and carrying me over to the big bed. I was glad my mother and father had renovated the upper floor of their house some years ago so there were several spacious guest bedrooms upstairs each with their own private bathroom. Fortunately for us, the rooms were far enough from the rest of the house so Albert and I could cavort and make love to our heart's delight without anyone downstairs hearing us.

I was laughing now and kissing his chest as he carried me towards the bed. "But I just had your baby, Albert."

"I know, I know," he said, laughing back, "but I want make another one – to make one in full consciousness of what I'm doing. Last time, I didn't realize at the time what was happening, even though I knew something powerful was taking place between us..."

We were on the bed now and he was smothering me playfully with kisses while I giggled.

"I can't explain it, but the thought of making you pregnant again is... well... just driving me crazy."

I lay back, enjoying his kisses. It was so wonderful when Albert was relaxed and happy like this and I was thankful that it was happening more and more frequently even though there were still times when he was obviously feeling great distress.

He was kissing my neck and between my breasts and then my breasts when he looked up and said, "It's like you've opened up a whole new world of sensations and feelings in me that I didn't know existed."

"I know what you mean," I said, running my fingers through his luscious black curls.

He stopped and sat up beside me, "But I'm serious, Rachel," he said solemnly. "Do you understand what I'm saying?"

The way he said that caught my attention. There was a strange note in his voice – almost one of desperation.

So I sat up too and said, "Saying... what?"

"That I want to make another baby with you?"

"Oh, Albert! Right now? Isabella isn't even two yet..."

When I said that, he groaned and put his head in his hands, "Oh, I know, I know! I'm so sorry, Rachel. What was I thinking? It must be the trauma talking. The doctor warned me this would happen..."

"Whatever do you mean?"

"Well, Lenny said it was important that I could distinguish between the rational, well-functioning part of me and the part of me that is still traumatized – and to be sure that I didn't let myself be controlled by or make decisions from the traumatized part of me. I think that's what just happened."

He leaned back against the headboard and took a few slow, deep breaths, trying to calm down.

After a few moments of deep breathing, he said, "Obviously I know with my rational mind that I just got back and that we don't need to rush into having another child right this very minute. So I guess it's the traumatized part of me that feels this immense desire and need to hold on to you and our love and our family... It's hard to explain, darling, it's just such a powerful feeling – almost a kind of desperation... and the thought of making your pregnant again... well... it's..."

"It's okay, darling," I said softly and took him in my arms. There were tears in his eyes. "It's okay, it's okay..."

We snuggled down together under the duvet and held each other tight. That's when I realized he was crying, no, sobbing actually. Great gut-wrenching sobs. It was the first time since his return that he'd cried like this. It was a deep, powerful wave of emotion and I knew that a great healing was taking place because he was finally letting out some of the terrible emotions that had been locked up inside him.

I didn't say a word but just held him.

A couple of weeks later, while my mother and I were standing by the window watching Albert cavorting with Isabella in the snow around one of the big old beech trees behind the house, she said to me, "Rachel, have you told him what Victor did to you?"

"No, Mother, I haven't," I replied softly.

"But you must," she said firmly. "He has to know."

"But the poor man's still so fragile – just think of what he's been through."

"I know, I know, my darling," she replied taking my hand, "but he is getting better every day, much better. Just look at him. Doctor Jacobs is working wonders with him."

We both smiled, watching Isabella squeal with delight as Albert put raisins for eyes and a carrot for a nose on the big snowman he was making for her.

When I didn't say anything, my mother continued, "You

simply can't keep putting it off, Rachel. You must tell him – you must. It would be one thing if the man wasn't connected to his business, but Victor is Albert's CEO and the Managing Director of his worldwide operations. Just think about it – that despicable man who raped and abused you so many times is the one the person in the world who has control of everything in Albert's business empire, and who's running the business right now. You can't know what kind of damage he's done to the business in Albert's absence. It's vitally important that you tell him before he calls Victor and tells him he's back."

I sighed because I knew she was right. I couldn't keep putting it off.

"I know it's going to be difficult, my darling, and I know you want to spare him from more emotional trauma, but he simply must know. Can't you see how much he loves and adores you and little Isabella? If there is anything that can really bring him completely back to life, I promise you, it will be having to defend and protect you and her. And besides, justice must be done!"

"Alright, Momma, but it's going to break his heart and infuriate him."

"I know," she sighed, "I know, but you've also been through a terrible trauma yourself and the man you love doesn't even know yet."

Even though I knew she was right, I kept putting it off. Maybe it was because Albert still sometimes had bad nightmares, or episodes of waking in the night in terror and not knowing where he was. All I wanted was to give him a little more time, a little more time to find his footing again, even though it was obvious that, slowly, slowly, he was getting better. Still I just didn't want to say or do anything that would jeopardize his recovery.

But then, four or five days later, Albert said to me as we were getting into bed for the night, "Rachel, I think I'm about ready to call Victor and my other managers and tell them I'm back. You know I can't hide out here at your mother's house forever."

When I heard Victor's name, it sent chills up and down my spine.

"Oh, can't we just wait a little longer, my darling? It's doing you so much good just being here like this. I can see it."

"I know, I know," he said, "but it's already February and we've been here for almost three months now. I can't keep putting it off forever."

We got into bed and he put his arms around me and pulled me close to him, kissing me on the cheek and ear. It was obvious he was gaining weight and feeling better. So I pinched him playfully in the ribs and said teasingly, "You're even getting a little fatter!"

We both laughed; enjoying the miracle of being together again after all we'd been through. Then he said, "Sweetheart, you never told me what happened between you and Victor that made you leave Cap Ferrat."

I felt myself stiffening even though I was trying to act natural.

"When I asked Stefan what happened," he continued, "all he would say was that it was best if I heard it from you. At the time, I thought it was typical Stefan – you know the man never says very much. But now that I'm beginning to relax and feel better, I know there's more to it."

When I didn't say anything, he added, "You know Victor is the CEO of my entire enterprise and he's been running the whole show for years and years. So Rachel, I must know what happened between you and him."

"That's exactly what my mother said," I said and burst out crying.

"Oh, darling," he said, holding me close, "it can't be that bad."

"Oh yes it can," I whispered softly. "You have no idea."

"Really?" He turned my head towards his and looked me deeply in the eyes. "Whatever it is, Rachel, I must know before I call him."

"Yes," I replied slowly. "I know I have to tell you. It's just so difficult."

"Well, just take your time, my love, and start at the beginning. I'm not going anywhere. Everyone is asleep now so we have all the time in the world."

He held me tightly to him again and said, "Now tell me, darling. From the beginning..."

"From the beginning?" I said, clearing my throat and trying to find the courage to speak. "Well, it all started after Jacques Durand from the Foreign Ministry called me at the end of June and told me that they'd lost all contact with the people who had abducted you, and that I should prepare myself for the worst!" I began to cry at the thought of it.

"My poor darling..." Albert whispered softly.

"Oh, darling," I continued as he dried my eyes gently, "you just can't imagine how awful that was for me! Up until then, well the government officials kept telling us that they were talking to your captors and that they'd asked for five million Euros in ransom and that, well... everything was going according to plan. According to them, that was how things worked in cases like yours when a rich businessman was abducted. Usually the captors are just out for the money so I had hope that you were alive because you were their ticket to the money. But when Jacques Durand said all communications had stopped..."

"Yes," said Albert softly, smoothing my hair, "and then what happened, darling?"

"Well... about four or five weeks later, Victor called, and asked me to come down to the annex because he had some news. I got all excited when he said that and dropped everything and ran down there. When I walked in, he said he was hopeful that serious negotiations with your kidnappers would soon be underway again. I was so delighted but also surprised and asked him how come Jacques Durand hadn't called me. He said it was because these negotiations were not through the Foreign Ministry but through private channels."

"Private channels? Hmmm. Did he say who these private

channels were?"

"Yes, he said it was through the Saudi Prince Abdul, the one you were in Jordan with. So of course, I was overjoyed. But then he said, I had to keep it secret and not tell anyone – and when I asked him why, all he would say was that was how the Prince wanted it. Obviously, I agreed. But then a few days later…" I said hesitantly.

I didn't want to go on; I felt my heart pounding in my chest.

"Yes, a few days later…" said Albert, trying not to be impatient with me. "What happened a few days later?"

When I didn't reply, Albert said again, ever so softly, "Come darling, you can tell me…"

I took a deep breath and plunged on, "Well, Victor asked me to come to the annex again, and again I ran down there hoping he would have some news about you. But this time he asked me to sit down because he said he wanted to discuss my situation at the house. Of course, I was surprised and didn't know what he was talking about. After I sat down, he went on to explain in a very businesslike manner that I really had no official status in relationship to you, and that actually I had no legal right to be there at all. And the only reason I was still living up in the big house was because of his kindness."

"What?!" cried Albert in surprise.

"Of course I was surprised and furious. So I jumped up and said, didn't he realize that you and I were in love and that we had a child together? But when I said that he just laughed and told me I was just another one of the many women who'd been after you over the years. And that in fact, he said, I was just a gold digger like the rest. He made me so furious, I told him you'd asked me to marry you the night before you left for Jordan, but again he just laughed and said that was an incredible story that no one would ever believe."

"Asshole!" cried Albert, who was getting more and more furious as my tale unfolded. "Of all the mean, low-down, rotten things to do! I ought to wring his neck!"

"But there's more," I whispered softly.

"More?" Albert asked in surprise.

"Yes, darling, it gets worse."

"Oh no," he said softly and went silent.

When I didn't speak, he said firmly, "Okay, Rachel, tell me the rest; come on now, tell me! I must know." There was a firmness in his voice, a new determination to hear it all, so I continued, understanding there was no turning back now.

"After I told Victor what I thought of him and turned to leave, Victor said, 'Not so fast, Rachel' – there was just one other thing he wanted to discuss with me. But I didn't turn around and kept heading for the door. And that was when he shouted at me, 'Rachel, who's going to pay the five million Euros in ransom for Albert's release if I don't. Do you have the money? Do you?' When I heard those awful words, I simply froze on the spot. I didn't know what to do. Then he told me to come back and sit down next to him. Oh Albert, it was awful, it was so awful!"

I gasped for air – and forced myself to go on.

"Then after I sat down, Victor said the negotiations for your release were going well, but that I had to have sex with him or else he wouldn't pay the ransom money they were demanding for your release!!!!"

"Oh, my God," cried Albert in disbelief. "Oh, my God!"

"And not only that I had to let him do it, but that I had to cooperate... and do it whenever and however he wanted it... and then he started touching me, right then and there..."

"Oh, my God," cried Albert again, "oh, my God!"

Then more of the story came out, and I wailed and cried as I told it, and Albert sat as if turned to stone.

When I was done, Albert held me for a long time and let me cry.

Then, as my sobbing subsided, there was silence. Neither of us moved or said a word for quite a while.

Finally Albert broke the silence and said in a very soft voice, "Why didn't you tell Stefan or call the police, my darling?" He was stroking my hair ever so gently, giving me time.

"Of course, my first thought was to tell Stefan, but Victor had sent him away on a very long business trip throughout the whole of the Middle East to – as he said – reassure all your business connections and partners that even though you were gone, it would be business as usual."

"The bastard!" exclaimed Albert.

"Yes, he'd thought it all through and knew that Stefan was the only person I really knew and trusted there on Cap Ferrat. As for the police, well I thought about that too, but then I realized it would just be my word against his. And who would believe me? Nobody! I had no proof! I didn't know a soul and he was your CEO and respected, longtime business associate – so why believe me? In their eyes, I would probably be just another one of the many women who really were after you."

"And your mother?"

"She was in hospital after having had a really hard time helping my sister through her nervous breakdown and suicide attempt, so I didn't dare tell her – she was so fragile. But when I imagined talking to her in my head, I knew she would have said I had no choice. If having sex with Victor was what it took to save you…" And with that, I broke down crying again. As I sobbed, I felt Albert's arms around me; but now they were as hard as steel. Slowly, slowly, my sobbing subsided and it was again very quiet in the room.

"I can see I wasn't the only one being held captive," Albert muttered almost to himself, but I heard him.

"Yes," I said, sniffing and wiping my nose, "I remember thinking the very same thing – that we were both being held captive by maniacs."

"But how did it end? I mean how did you finally get away?"

"It was Claudia," I said slowly, realizing that I would have to tell Albert even more about the degradation I suffered.

"Claudia?"

"Yes, Claudia Raffin. You know, Madam Raffin?"

"Oh, her," he said, "I didn't know who you were talking about. What about her?"

"Well, it started the night she prepared me for Victor."

"Prepared you?"

"Yes, he wanted something extra special that night so she bathed me and corseted me and painted my nipples red – all the things that really turned him on… "

"Prepared you?! My God, Rachel," cried Albert fiercely, no longer able to contain himself, "we're taking about rape! RAPE!"

He was so furious he jumped up from the bed and roared to the heavens, "Oh, how I'd like to kill the bastard! Kill him!"

Now he was pacing back and forth at the foot of the bed like a lion in a cage. "And Claudia was in cahoots with him! I can't believe it!"

"Yes, or so I thought, until later that night… You see, after it was all over… and I'd gone back to the house… I collapsed on our bed and was crying my heart out, when – to my great surprise – Claudia came in and comforted me. That was when I found out she really hated Victor too. Do you know what happened between him and her – because she absolutely detests the man?"

Albert stopped to think. I could see he was really trying to control himself. Talking about Claudia seemed a helpful distraction for the moment, so he said slowly, "No, I'm not really sure but I do know she was a prostitute when she was very young – apparently from the mean streets of Marseilles. But how he met her I don't actually know. All I know is that he picked her up somewhere when they were both very young – and as far as I remember, she had a serious drug problem. I think he helped her get clean and had some kind of hold over her – I never quite found out exactly what it was. But that's why she started working at our house – because of Victor. She was already working there when I came back from Japan."

He was quiet for a moment and then started pacing the room again.

"But then what happened, Rachel? What did you do?"

"Well, up until that night, Claudia thought I was having sex with Victor because I wanted to. But when she heard what really happened, how he'd blackmailed me, she was absolutely livid. So that's how she became my ally.

"It also turned out that she had been secretly recording Victor's conversations in his office to protect herself if he turned against her – so she had a recording of Victor's conversation with me. The one where he blackmailed me into sleeping with him, which meant we had proof. Proof! And could go to the police!

"But it was the weekend then and Claudia didn't think we should go to the police until Monday because she wanted us to talk to someone at a very high level – and not just some ordinary policeman who was on duty during the weekend. I thought that made sense, also because Victor was gone on business and said he wouldn't be back until the middle of the week. So we decided to go to the police first thing Monday morning. But then Victor surprised us and returned unexpectedly to the house from Germany on Sunday afternoon... And he had that brute, Felix, with him – and they both wanted to fuck me..."

Albert stopped pacing and just stood there, staring at me as if he had seen a ghost.

"My first impulse when I saw them drive up to the house was to run away, but Claudia was there with me and she was afraid that Victor might harm the children if I did... so I didn't dare..."

"Harm the children!" cried Albert, holding his head in his hands. "Harm our little baby... Oh, my God... NO!!"

By now Albert was in an absolute rage. I don't think I'd ever seen him so furious.

But he didn't say another word; instead he just paced back and forth like a trapped animal as I finished the story, including how

Prince Abdul finally called and told me the truth about Victor just as I was going back to the House of Sin for that last terrible night of degradation with Victor and Felix.

When I was done, Albert just stood there, staring at me in complete and utter horror.

Then he took a very deep breath and got back into bed next to me. He took me in his arms and held me. All he could say was, "My poor baby... my poor baby..." Then he smoothed down my hair and held me tight until I fell asleep. And he kept on holding me the whole night. Every time I woke up, we were still in the exact same position. He was just sitting there, holding me tightly and staring into the darkness. I don't think he slept a wink that night. All he did was sit there and hold me and think, the whole night through.

In the morning he was a changed man – fierce, galvanized.

And he wasn't smiling.

After I'd taken my morning shower, I found him in the kitchen talking quietly to my mother.They had their backs turned to me so they didn't see me come in. He had his arm around her shoulder and I knew they'd been talking about me. I could just feel it. I tiptoed over to them and heard Albert saying, "I'm going to need your office, Isabel. I have work to do, lots of work – and there's not a moment to lose."

But then the floor creaked and they heard me and turned around, opening their arms wide to receive me – and the three of us embraced. No one said a word. No words were necessary. We just stood there, holding each other tightly, Albert, my mother and me. It was truly heartwarming to feel their love.

For almost three days and nights after that, we didn't see much of Albert; he was holed up in my mother's office talking almost constantly on the phone with his people or working on the computer. It was like the old Albert was back. Fierce, determined, focused. In fact, it was exactly as my mother had predicted it would be. Now that Albert knew his family had been under attack, he was ready to go into battle for us. And into battle he went. The only break he took was when Isabella awoke from her afternoon nap – then he'd take an hour and play with her. Either outside on the grounds around my mother's house or on the floor in the living room.

On the third evening, he came out of my mother's office and joined my mother and I in the living room, after the children had been put to bed. He sat down on my father's favorite armchair, put his feet up on the ottoman, and took a deep breath. Then he said, "Well, it looks like everything is in place now. We should have that bastard, Victor, neutralized and arrested by the end of the week."

"God, am I happy to hear that," cried my mother.

"Yeah, me too," I said softly. "But I don't know if I'll really believe it until it happens."

"Oh, it will happen, darling," replied Albert fiercely. "It will happen, I promise you!"

"Can you tell us a little about what you've been doing, Albert?"

"Sure. Well… even before I could start working with my lawyers to get Victor arrested, I had to deal with Victor's access to all the various parts of my business and to our finances and financial systems. Giovanni International is a worldwide enterprise and Victor is the only person – besides me – who has access to EVERYTHING – to our whole network. So before anything else, I had to make sure he could do no more damage once I made my move. That meant working with our IT team to block his access to all our systems, which took quite some doing.

"But thank God, we had the advantage that up until now, no one besides Stefan knew that I was back. It was funny, but when you weren't in Cap Ferrat, Rachel, I just knew something was terribly wrong. And when Stefan said you'd had some trouble with Victor, well I had a very bad feeling about it right from the start. But I guess I was still so much in shock that it really didn't register that I needed to move and move quickly. Anyway, it turned out to be a really good thing that Stefan and I decided to keep my return secret.

"As of now, my IT team has changed all Victor's passwords and blocked his access to all our systems and accounts – both customer accounts and financial accounts. God knows what other damage he may have done while I was gone, but we'll find out soon enough. My people are trawling through all our systems and accounts right now to see what's been going on."

"But won't he get suspicious if he can't access the system?" I asked.

"Yes, of course, but hopefully not right away. Victor already called Stefan in a panic this morning because he couldn't access the system. But Stefan was prepared and told him that Giovanni International had been hacked and was the target of a massive cyber attack. He told Victor that our IT team was dealing with the damage as they spoke. Stefan sent all the rest of our staff home, so that should hold Victor off for a little while at least – but not for long. Pretty soon he'll start getting suspicious, so I've also been working with my legal team, and my lawyers are going to file charges against him by the end of the week at the latest. I spoke to Claudia in Marseilles today – she sends you her love – and I sent a special team over to her to get the recordings. We need that as evidence. So everything is in place, my darl—"

But he didn't finish because his phone rang. Albert took it out of his pocket. "Oh, it's the Prince! I've been trying to get a hold of him all day," he said, standing up. "Excuse me, ladies, but I have to take this—" And with that he left the room.

My mother came over and sat next to me on the couch.

"It looks like Albert has everything under control again, Rachel," she said brightly. "And he seems so much better already – now that's he focused on taking care of you and his family."

"Yes, Momma, you were so right. He really does seem transformed. Almost like his old self again."

Half an hour later, Albert returned with the strangest look on his face. He didn't say anything but just sat down in my father's armchair again. He looked rather pleased with himself.

"Well, what did he say?" I asked, remembering how kind the Prince had been to me on the phone when I talked to him that fateful night in Cap Ferrat.

"A lot! You know the Prince and I have always been very close. I've known him for many years... He's here in New York at the moment..."

Then he was silent. But when he realized that my mother and I were still looking at him, waiting for his answer, he said slowly, "Well, I told him briefly about my captivity and escape and we agreed to meet soon. Then I told him what had happened to you, Rachel, while I was gone and the measures I was taking to neutralize Victor. I told him we were going to file charges by the end of this week and that we were planning on taking Victor to court and ruining him for good. The whole time I was talking about Victor, the Prince didn't say a word. He just listened, which is not like him at all. Usually he has a lot to say about everything. Anyway, when I was done, I said, 'I hope to God we have enough evidence to put that bastard away for a long, long time!' Then finally the Prince did speak – and he said, 'Don't you worry about the court case, Albert. I'll take care of Victor.' I was about to ask him what he meant by that when his other phone rang and he said he had to take the call. So he hung up and left me wondering what the hell he meant when he said he'd take care of Victor..."

Three days later we got our answer. My mother and I were eating lunch in the kitchen with Amélie and the children and CNN was on in the background. Suddenly we both noticed that one of the top stories of the day was about a car bombing in one of the finer suburbs of Vienna. A wealthy businessman by the name of Victor Gandler had been killed in a car bomb when he started his car to go to work at seven forty-five that morning. The authorities had no idea why Gandler was the target of such a brutal attack, and at the moment, no one had stepped forward to claim responsibility for it. Gandler, they said, was the CEO of Giovanni International, the same Giovanni International whose owner – Albert Giovanni – had been abducted by Islamic militants last December while he was attending a conference in Amman, Jordan and who was still missing. There was already some speculation that the two events might be connected in some way because the company had far-reaching dealings in many countries in the Middle East. But no one knew for sure.

My mother and I stopped eating at exactly the same moment but neither of us said a word. A few minutes later, Albert joined us for lunch looking unusually cheerful.

No one said anything.

When the children were finished eating, I asked Amélie to take Isabella and Daniel outside to play for a while since it was such a lovely day. When they were gone, my mother and I turned to Albert and I said, "Do you know what happened?"

"Yes, Stefan called me early this morning and told me…"

A few nights later after we'd gotten into bed, Albert said to me, "We have to go back to Cap Ferrat, darling. There's so much I need to do and I can't do it here."

I tensed up when I heard him say that, even though I knew it was coming.

"Oh I know you need to go… it's just…"

But he didn't let me finish. "I know what you're feeling, darling, believe me. I'm sure I'd feel the same if I had to go back to that hellhole in Yemen – so I've had the annex and the guest house torn down completely."

"You what?" I cried in surprise.

"I've had them torn down completely. In fact, they are already gone. Both buildings have been demolished. The annex and the guest house – both of them. By the time we get there, they will have planted new trees and grass will be growing where they once stood."

I just sat there, stunned. "You had it all torn down?"

"Yes," he said and then he added softly, "It will be as if those accursed buildings never existed!"

He was silent for a moment. "And it's not just for you, my darling; I never want to see those godforsaken buildings again either. Just the thought of them and what happened to you there makes my blood turn cold. But now they're all gone and so is that despicable bastard!"

When I didn't reply, he took me in his arms and softly smoothed down my hair which was strewn all over the place. "I've asked your mother to come with us too because I am sure that will make it easier for you. And she's already said yes."

"But... I was hoping we could live here in New York," I said softly. "We do have the loft and I've already enrolled at NYU."

"I know, I know, my darling, and I wish we could, but it's just not feasible right now. We can come back here in the fall when school begins if you want, I promise. But right now, there's just so much I have to set straight again after that bastard – and I can only do that from Cap Ferrat. I need to have all my people around me for a while. Please understand, darling. I've already been away for more than a year now."

When he saw the tears on my cheeks, he wiped them away softly and said, "Rachel, I love you so much – I promise you, nothing bad is going to happen to you there ever again, nothing."

"But what if you have to go away on business?" I cried. "What then? I don't ever want to be there in that house on my own again... I don't..."

"Rachel, darling, if it will make you feel any better, I promise you I won't go anywhere – not even on business – without you. So if I have to go anywhere... well... then you and Isabella will just have to go with me. But as for me... I don't think I could be parted from you and little Isabella at the moment anyway. Really. Not after all we've been through. I simply don't think I could manage it – even if I wanted to. So it's not going to happen. You have my word."

I sat quietly for a moment, contemplating how my life would be there, and then I blurted out, "But you're going to be so busy."

"And so are you," he replied immediately.

"Me? Doing what?"

"Well I've set up a foundation, Rachel, and I've named it the ISG Fund – after our daughter, Isabella Somers Giovanni – to help women in the Middle East in their struggle for freedom."

"Really?"

"Yes, really! Remember how we've talked about how we wanted to find a way to help Safa and other women like her in Yemen and the other countries where women are struggling for freedom and the right to an education?

"Well, I told you I would find a way, and now after talking to the experts, I've come to the conclusion that setting up a foundation would be a good vehicle for this kind of work. So we have a forum which can work actively to support women's rights and education in those countries. And Rachel, I want you to be the head of the foundation – to run it."

"Me?" I cried in surprise.

"Yes, you. I can't do it all by myself – and besides, I have Giovanni International to run at the moment."

"But I don't know how to run a foundation!"

"I know," he said laughing, "but you're smart, Rachel, and you'll learn and you'll figure it out."

I was silent for a while, trying to digest what he'd just said. Sometimes the man truly amazed me.

"And I'll be there to help you."

When I still didn't reply he added, "Besides, didn't you say you wanted to do something to help women?"

"Yes, of course," I said softly, thinking about how Safa had saved Albert's life. "I really, really do. Nothing would make me happier than to find a way to somehow repay Safa – even just a little – for her amazing courage and bravery."

"And what about your mother?" he continued. "She'll be there too and she's smart and dynamic and needs something positive to do as well. So she can help you."

"My mother?"

"Yes, your mother. Just think about it, Rachel. In the same way that being a mother isn't enough for you, well, just being a grand-mother isn't enough for her either. I am sure she would be thrilled to be a part of something like this."

"Yes," I said slowly, thinking about what he said. "Of course, you're right. It would be wonderful for her, especially now that my father's gone. I know she feels her life is pretty empty when we're not here."

So we talked on into the night. And as we did, I felt a little smile creeping into my soul as I listened to all Albert's plans and dreams for us. It was as if more and more of the old Albert was back. More and more of my old, wonderful, wise, self-confident, self-contained, brilliant Albert was back. Which made me smile inside and feel happier than I'd felt in a long, long time.

That was why I sighed, because it looked like I would be going back to Cap Ferrat after all, even though I vowed never to set foot there again. It was obvious that Albert had thought it all through and had made up his mind. But even though I was smiling inwardly, I had to pout a little – just for show. But inside, the truth was, I was overjoyed and knew in my heart of hearts that I loved him and would follow him anywhere.

So I just sat there, listening to him and looking at him and glowing inwardly.

And he just sat there too, sharing his dreams and explaining his plans to me and allowing me to catch up with him.

When he was all done, I chuckled and said, "Well, at least Daniel will be happy! He's been pestering me about going back to

Cap Ferrat since the moment we arrived here in New York. He misses his best friend Simon and the other kids he went to playschool with."

"Yeah, I know, he's asked me the very same question every day since I got back," said Albert, with a twinkle in his eye, because he knew it was my way of saying I would follow him no matter what.

We sat for a while in silence, listening to the wind in the trees outside and the old clock ticking on the wall.

It was so nice and peaceful; I felt so safe and knew that Albert did too, at least for the moment.

Then Albert added softly as if he didn't really want to break the spell of contentment we were feeling, "There's just one other thing, my darling, just one other thing. I'm going to have to come out of hiding soon and go public about my escape. When that happens, there's going to be a lot of media attention. So I've hired a security team to protect us – and the French Foreign Ministry will be involved too. I know it's going to be hectic for a while - so we'll just have to ride out the storm. But compared to what we've already been through, I'm sure we'll survive."

And with that, he pulled me too him in the bed and unbuttoned the big shirt of his I was wearing so he could see and touch my body. Then he began tracing his finger slowly down to my belly and around my navel. "Do you remember the very first night we met and made love?"

I knew he was trying to distract me from my fears and worries but I had to admit, I didn't mind. In fact, I wanted to be distracted, especially by him…

"Do you remember how intense it was?" he said softly as his finger moved slowly across my bare belly. His touch felt tantalizingly gentle and altogether lovely.

Yes, I nodded, I remembered.

"The night we made Isabella?"

Yes, I nodded again, yes, I remembered.

"The night I fell in love with you… because you know I did, my darling, I really did fall in love with you that very first night. Passionately, insanely in love with you…"

Now he was leaning over me and kissing my breasts softly. I felt my breath quicken. There was just something about the way he touched me. He just knew what to do.

"And I'm still passionately in love with you," he said slowly, looking at me with such love and devotion.

It was like he was back.

It was like he was whole again, at least for the moment.

And it was like I was too. Back and whole again, at least for the moment. And we were both relishing the feeling of it – the intensity of it. Of being together again now, in this moment. And of remembering the night we met and reconnecting with that energy. The powerful energy that was released between us the very first night we met. Because powerful it was, indeed. And powerful it continued to be, right up until this very day.

I felt myself smiling even though just a little while ago I'd been in despair at the thought of going back to the house on Cap Ferrat again. But now I didn't care.

No I didn't care – as long as I could be with Albert.

I put my fingers in his hair and felt its wonderful thickness. The same jet black, wavy hair that little Isabella had.

He was kissing my belly now and moving slowly down to my pussy and already she was feeling all liquidy at the thought of him approaching. Because he had those amazing lips and that amazing tongue and he could use them in that very special way that was so intensely pleasurable. And he knew it. Knew he could do things to me that no man had ever done before… because he had this skill, this quality and he could take his time and wait and pleasure me, knowing all the while that his time would come too. That was how one-pointed his attention could be.And now he was doing it to me again, focusing on me with that one-point-edness that could only take me to new and ever more blissful heights. And I heard myself sighing and sinking down into the bed and into pleasure of allowing him to take me and possess me. Yes, sinking down into the blissfulness of letting myself surrender to this amazing man and all the amazing sensations he could awaken in me.

"Oh, Albert," I sighed and let go of his head and his wonderful hair and surrendered to him as Ihad done in the very beginning, on that fateful night in Nice some two and a half years ago.

His tongue, his masterful tongue, was now caressing the delicate lips of my pussy and she was opening to him like a flower, blooming and blossoming, and I felt my hips swaying ever so slightly as I sighed and sang and allowed him to see me and own me and love me...

And then, just as I was about to come, he pulled back and mounted me and penetrated me so gently and deeply that my wet pussy felt all the deliciousness of his manhood and his powerful desire for me. And then I knew it – knew that nothing – nothing whatsoever – could possibly be more magnificent or more pleasurable than to be loved by the man you loved. Nothing could possibly be better than this... nothing...

And so I cried, "Oh, Albert!"

And he met me there, crying back, "Yes, my darling! Yes!"

And we were singing and sighing together, like the wind in the trees, like the spring and the summer in the grass, like the... and then it happened. The liquid desire between us came thundering in and it overpowered us and we both exploded and came, yes we both came and we came, and we both came home... together... at the very same moment, finally together. Together at last!

Romance, erotica, sensual or downright ballsy. When you want to escape: whether seeking a passionate fulfilment, a moment behind the bike sheds, a laugh with a chick-lit or a how-to – come into the Bedroom and take your pick. Bedroom readers are open-minded explorers knowing exactly what they like in their quest for pleasure, delight, thrills or knowledge.